Grange Hill After Hours

Also available in Magnet
Tucker in Control

PHIL REDMOND

Grange Hill After Hours

Based on the BBC Television Series
GRANGE HILL

A Magnet Book

First published 1986 as a Magnet paperback
by Methuen Children's Books Ltd
11 New Fetter Lane, London EC4P 4EE
Text copyright and TV format © Philip Redmond 1986
Cover photographs copyright © BBC Enterprises 1986

Printed in Great Britain
by Richard Clay (The Chaucer Press) Ltd,
Bungay, Suffolk

ISBN 0 416 64640 9

ONE

It's a cracker, this, thought Ziggy, as he lay awake on his bed leafing through the latest edition of one of his mum's magazines. Well, it wasn't really the magazine that he was so pleased about. Ziggy didn't really want to know how to make yesterday's left-overs stretch for two days. He couldn't even think why his mum needed to know as she had been doing an excellent job for as long as he could remember. He wasn't even interested in how to get different types of stains out of his clothes, although he was an expert at putting them there. Ziggy certainly wasn't interested in the knitting patterns, although he did glance twice at the girl advertising tights on page 38. No, what Ziggy was really pleased about was that he was off school. That is, he was pleased until he moved.

'Aaagghh!' he groaned as the pain came back and with it the memory of Imelda Davis. Stupid bitch, thought Ziggy as he eased himself on to his side. He still couldn't understand why she had done it.

I mean, he thought, I might have snotted her once and shoved her in that fountain, but . . . bloody 'ell there was no need for her to lose her rag and shove fibreglass down me back, was there. I wonder why, he mused. She could have just smacked me with a brush or something rather than this. Must have something missing upstairs. She looks all right . . . doesn't look like a cabbage head. Must be, though. She was messing about with that frog in Assembly on the first day and all, wasn't she. Wonder she didn't eat it.

Ziggy shifted position once again and finally managed to get comfortable as he eased himself down on to the extra pillow his mum had given him for his back.

When Imelda had shoved fibreglass down his shirt it had badly scratched his back and the doctor had said he should stay at home for a few days to allow it time to heal. To help him his mum had given him an extra pillow as a cushion. It worked well until he moved: then his back felt as though there was six kittens clawing their way up it. However, when he was still and comfortable everything was bearable. Especially as he didn't have to go to Grange Hill.

Ziggy hadn't complained about being told to stay off school, just as he had refused to tell anyone how he had ended up with fibreglass down his back. He didn't need anyone to fight his battles for him. He would sort out Imelda when he went back which, at the moment, he wanted to keep as far in the future as possible. Ziggy was not happy at the prospect of returning.

It wasn't simply a case of not liking Grange Hill, or even not liking school. Ziggy didn't mind. He didn't mind much in life, taking everything as it came and being able to find a good laugh in most things. The problem for Ziggy was that he was lonely. Like a lot of people, Ziggy mixed with the twelve hundred pupils of Grange Hill but found he was a stranger. An outsider. A lonely figure in a vast crowd.

He kept reminding himself of what his dad had told him when he first started. 'It's normal,' his dad would say. 'Everyone feels strange at first. Everyone *is* strange at first. And no one talks because no one wants to either make a show of themselves or risk feeling soft if no one speaks to them. It just takes time to get to know each other.' He could remember it almost word for word. His dad had given him a pep-talk the night before Ziggy was going to start at Grange Hill. It had to be the night before because ever since the family had moved down from Liverpool his dad had had to work nights.

Mind you, his dad didn't complain, as this job was the first he'd had since losing his previous one four years before. As there was no chance of work in Liverpool or anywhere else in the North, Ziggy's dad had travelled south and been fortunate enough to find a job in a car factory. Ziggy wasn't sure what he did, but when he left for school in the morning his dad was usually still in bed and when he got home his dad had gone to work. Ziggy had hardly seen him since he started at Grange Hill, but he could still hear his voice giving him the pep-talk, ending with the words 'And remember, lad. If you're feeling like a right Herbert – so is everyone else! You're all the same under the skin.'

Perhaps under the skin, thought Ziggy. But right now I wish someone else had mine. He slowly repositioned himself on the pillow, took another glance at the girl advertising tights on page 38 and let his mind wander back to his worries about Grange Hill.

It's not being on my own. At least I don't think so. I know I'll get to know people, like . . . but . . . oh, I don't know. I suppose I miss the other two.

He then turned and looked across at what passed as a dressing table, which was in fact four cardboard boxes still full of stuff he hadn't bothered to unpack

7

since the move. On top of the cardboard boxes was an old piece of kitchen worktop on which was propped a mirror, an old radio-cassette and various other pieces of junk. Ziggy could no longer remember why he kept them, but refused to throw them out – just in case! His mum was particularly keen to throw out an old, and even Ziggy had to admit, mangey stuffed squirrel. He had bought it for 50p at a school jumble sale in Liverpool, mainly because his great rival Bomber Lassiter had wanted it. Since then it had always had pride of place in his bedroom, more so because his mum hated it. Anyway, standing next to the squirrel was a framed picture of himself – flanked on either side by his two sisters Michelle and Allison. He hated to admit it, but he missed them both.

Michelle was fifteen and in her 'O' level year and Allison was seventeen and in her 'A' level year. When Mum and Dad had decided to move the family south they decided not to disrupt the girls and let them stay with their Auntie Ann. As Ziggy was about to change schools anyway it made sense for him to move south as well.

Ziggy looked at the girl on page 38 of the magazine. She looked like Allison. It was her he missed the most. Michelle was more of a pain in the bum. But he couldn't remember how many times he had fallen asleep on Allie's knee, when he was still a kid. And she was always there to help, even when Mum wasn't.

Huh, he thought, until she started going out with that spotty bloke from the Building Society. What was his name ... oh yeah ... Dennis. Once she met him she was never in then, was she?

Ziggy remembered an almighty row one night back

home when Allison had come home late and Dad had had a real go at her. Ziggy remembered it was a real old ding-dong about 'who did she think she was?' and 'what time of night do you call this?' Dad even hit Allison for arguing and everyone was shocked.

Dad had never hit any of them before, but it wasn't until the next day that they all found out why. Dad announced that he had found a job but it was down south. He knew it meant splitting up the family and he was naturally worried about what would happen to the girls if 'this was the way they were going to carry on'. Allison had apologised and they all made it up, but the shock of splitting up the family was greater than Dad hitting Allison.

That's what it is, thought Ziggy as he found himself once more on page 38. I'm lonely because I'm missing the girls. I don't mind being alone at school. Da's right. I'll soon make new friends, but, well, at home you need someone to talk to, don't you. Someone other than your parents, like. God, it drives me mental sometimes. Specially with me da always working. Ma's OK, but . . . well she tends to talk about the same things all the time, doesn't she. The house, keeping me room tidy, price of stuff and having nowhere to go. Suppose she's lonely, too. Most women must be. They all talk about the same things. And read the same old magazines!

He took one last look at the legs on page 38, dropped the magazine on the floor and looked over at the Mickey Mouse alarm clock – which had half the big finger missing as a result of throwing it at his sister Michelle last Christmas Eve. It was nearly four o'clock. Everyone would have left Grange Hill by now and his mum would be back from the shops soon. He eased himself into a sitting position. He needed to go to the loo. Still, he thought, as he made his way slowly across the landing to the toilet, it's better than double English. If only I had someone to talk to!

TWO

Somebody who didn't have to worry about having someone to talk to was Julia Glover. She was now in the third year at Grange Hill, although it was her first term there. This was because she used to go to Grange Hill's old rival, Brookdale. However, the two schools, together with another comprehensive, Rodney Bennett, had merged into one. Suddenly people who had been sworn enemies and rivals found themselves mixing in the same corridors and class-rooms. Some were even sitting next to each other. However, Julia had no such fears as she had stayed with her best friend Laura Reagan through it all. Unlike Ziggy, they didn't have to worry about lone-liness. They had each other. Sometimes, however, Laura wished they hadn't. Like now. Julia was once again wittering on about her father. She never stopped, thought Laura, although I can't blame her. What a pain!

'God, I don't know how you put up with him,' Laura said, as they turned up the garden path that led to Julia's front door.

'I don't have much choice, do I?' Julia responded.

'Yes, you do. Don't tell him things!'

'I can't do that,' insisted Julia.

'Why not? He'll only drone on and on . . . and on . . . and on . . . and on. . . .'

'All right. There's no need for you to act like him.'

'Well, he only does it because he knows what you're

up to, doesn't he? If you didn't tell him, he wouldn't know. So?' Laura let the thought hang in the air.

'He'll want to know. He always does. He makes sure he knows every little detail. Right down to how many times I go to the loo when I'm out.'

'Oh, well in that case,' offered Laura. She was not going to be beaten by Mr Glover. 'In that case you'll have to lie. If he can't treat you like an adult, he'll have to be treated like a child, won't he?'

'Easier said than done,' muttered Julia as she opened the door into the kitchen.

There was no sign of Julia's mother, so the two girls dumped their bags and set about the fridge and teapot to keep them going until the evening meal.

'Toast?' offered Julia.

Laura nodded. As she threw the tea bags from the teapot down the sink she turned to Julia. 'I can understand that he's not keen on you going to Louise Webb's party, but . . . well, I can't understand why he won't let you go to the Jumble Sale tonight.'

'Same reason. It's "after hours", isn't it? There might be boys there.' Julia laughed.

'Oh my God – no! Not boys!' Laura fell into a chair acting as though the shock was too much for her. This, at last, finally managed to bring a smile to Julia's lips. 'Your dad's first name isn't Walter by any chance, is it?' asked Laura suddenly.

'No,' Julia responded, a little puzzled. 'No, it's Martin.'

'Oh . . . it's just that . . . well, he sounds like a right wally, doesn't he?'

Julia smiled and threw the tea-towel at Laura. 'You can be so stupid at times.'

'I know. But life's like that, isn't it?'

'Yeah, I suppose so. Do you want jam on your toast?'

Laura nodded as she poured the boiling water from the kettle to the teapot. 'You've told Louise you're going to the party, haven't you?'

'Yeah. Don't know how, though.'

'Never mind that. We'll think of something nearer the time. It's the Jumble Sale we have to crack first.' Laura thought about it a bit more as she moved toward the kitchen door to go to the loo. 'Are you definitely sure his name's not Walter?' she asked as she nipped through the door into the hall, just in time to dodge a piece of low-flying toast.

Julia walked across to retrieve the missile. Laura's right, though, she thought as she moved back to the grill. He does go over the top, doesn't he. What harm is there in going to something so . . . so . . . so ordinary . . . so *boring* as a Jumble Sale?

She thought back for a moment over all the trouble she'd had with her father. He had always been a pain. Laura was right about that, too. But it had got worse over the last few years, as she had grown up. God, he still treats me like a kid, Julia thought as she punched a hole in the top of a new jar of jam. She knew she didn't really have to do it. She could have prised it off, or just turned it to break the seal, but she knew it annoyed her father. It was the same with the milk bottles. She would deliberately poke a hole into the silver foil top. He hated it. The more he ranted and raved the more she 'forgot' to take it off properly. If the milkman didn't leave the usual bottles, she would do the same with the cartons. She would open them on the wrong side. She chuckled to herself as she remembered how mad he had got one day when she

13

had used the bread knife to saw open a carton of orange juice instead of using the scissors. He had tried to grab the carton from her and in so doing had squeezed the sides. The result was orange juice squirting all over the kitchen floor and better still, all over the front of his shirt. Everyone, even Steve her older brother, had found it funny, but no one had dared laugh until he had gone to change.

This is ridiculous, she suddenly thought. What am I doing standing here giggling to myself about how many ways I know to irritate my own father. It is. It's ridiculous. But he does ask for it. Pompous idiot. If only – if only he'd be more – more understanding . . . more tolerant.

She was snapped out of her thoughts by Laura's voice as she came back into the room. 'Penny for your thoughts.'

'Not worth that much.'

'That boring, eh?'

'Yeah. I was just wondering . . . well, I was just wondering why my dad carries on like he does.'

'He's an idiot, isn't he?'

'Oh, come on, Laura. He's still my dad, you know.'

'Sorry,' offered Laura, as she moved across the kitchen to pour two mugs of tea. 'He's just being over-protective, isn't he. Mum was the same just after she and dad got divorced.' Laura rolled her eyes at the thought. 'God, she was terrible. I couldn't even walk down the road to the shops by myself, because she'd be a basket case by the time I got back. I don't know what she thought was going to happen in two hundred yards!'

'A lot of children have gone missing in less,' Julia

replied. 'Remember that boy who disappeared on his way home from school last year? He was found dead six weeks later, wasn't he?'

'I know, but . . .' Laura shrugged, then adopted the pose she always took to imitate Bridget McCluskey, the school's Deputy Head, one hand on her hip, the other wagging her finger. 'So long as you follow the rules and don't talk to strangers. . . .'

'Or let people do what you don't like!' chipped in Julia, now warming to the theme.

'And never be afraid to shout!' added Laura, moving closer to Julia as the two girls shouted the final line of their routine. 'Then you won't have to worry!!!'

They were still giggling as they sat down on the thick fluffy rug that almost filled Julia's bedroom. This is nice, thought Laura as she slowly pulled her fingers through the deep pile of the rug. Julia's father might be a right pain. But at least he's still around to cough up for this sort of thing. She knew that was a little unfair on her own father, as he did his best to try and help out. She had never really understood what had happened between her mother and father to cause the divorce, but she knew they were both happier living apart. They both still talked to each other; which was better than some of the kids at school. Some of them never even saw their fathers. Some of them weren't allowed to by their mothers! Stupid, thought Laura. If they can't speak to each other they shouldn't try and stop the kids talking to their own parents. She saw her father whenever she wanted to and he did his best to help out, whenever and wherever he could.

She looked round the room as Julia rummaged

through a stack of cassettes. Far more than Laura had. Her stereo cassette radio was better as well. And she had a television, even if it was only an old black and white set. I wonder how much all this was, Laura thought as she noticed the dressing table and matching wardrobe and bedside cabinets. It must cost an absolute fortune to kit out a whole house like this. Whatever Julia's father's like, at least he's here to pay for it. She then thought back to her own bedroom. Although she too had a wardrobe and dressing table, they were old and tatty. She certainly didn't have a television, let alone a rug like the one she was now curling her toes into. She also began to realise what a difficult job it must be for her own mother and father. They didn't just have one house to fill and run, but two – one for her father and one for her mother.

She'd never really thought about it before. She had noticed that when her father left he had taken some of the furniture. Especially that big old armchair she liked to curl up in to watch the telly. She missed that, although she enjoyed using it when she stayed over at her father's. She had also noticed that most of father's 'new' furniture, was in fact 'old'. She had even been with him a couple of times to the secondhand shops looking for bits and pieces.

I bet that's how I got interested in Jumble Sales, Laura thought, as she tried to scrape off a drop of jam from the front of her skirt, but only succeeded in spreading the stain. It's all the years going round junk shops with my father. He's got me interested now.

'What are you grinning about?' Laura suddenly heard Julia say.

'Oh . . . I was just thinking about my dad,' Laura replied.

'Must have been funny, then.'

'Not really. I was just thinking about the times I'd been round junk shops with him.'

'Sounds hilarious,' Julia commented, with a touch of sarcasm in her voice.

'It can be, sometimes. Especially if he starts to argue about the price of something. I remember once, he wanted some old clock. And he was convinced the guy who was selling it was asking too much. So dad told him and offered him half the price.'

'What did the guy say?'

'What do you think he said?'

'I can imagine,' said Julia.

'Anyway, they started to haggle about it, but it soon grew into an outright argument with the guy accusing Dad of being an old miser and Dad accusing the guy of being a robber. They even started pushing each other back and forth and tugging at the clock.'

'What happened?'

'The guy called his mate from the back and they threw Dad out – bonk! Right into the street.'

Julia was amazed 'What . . . was – was he all right?'

'Oh yes. I ran out, tears running down my cheeks because these horrible men had hurt my daddy and the fool was lying on the pavement laughing his head off!'

'Why?'

Laura just shrugged. 'He just seemed to enjoy the row. That's one of the things why Mum says they split up. Still, I got the biggest ice-cream I've ever eaten out of it because he'd given me such a fright.'

'And you've got the nerve to ask me if my dad's name is Walter?' Julia asked, as she belted Laura with her old one-eyed teddy bear. 'And never mind you and your junk shops,' she added. 'What are we going to do about us and the Jumble Sale?'

'Don't you mean you and *your* Jumble Sale?' Laura corrected. 'I'm OK, I can go!'

Julia just pulled a face to say 'very funny!' She then added, 'But if your mum was as bad as my dad, how did you . . . I mean . . . how come things are all right now? How come she does let you go out?'

'I told you. I just didn't tell her. Well . . . at first.' Laura then grinned. 'Until she found out!'

'Then what?'

'We sat down and talked about it. I told her I was growing up and although I was still following all the rules, it'd be better for her to know about things rather than for me to do it behind her back.'

'What did she say?'

'Not much.' Laura paused, watching Julia's amazed look grow.

'Just like that?'

'Yeah . . . well . . . after she thumped me for telling lies, and then kept me in for three months.'

Julia gave Laura another belt with the teddy bear. 'You can be such an idiot at times.'

'I know, I take after my dad.'

'So what do I do between now and seven o'clock?'

'Tell lies!' Laura twisted to one side to avoid another attack by the one-eyed teddy.

Julia sat back and looked at her friend. Although Laura was being flippant about the situation, she was right. It was time for Julia to stand up to her father and tell him she was growing up and had to be treated as such. She then thought about what she would say. Then about what he would say. She nodded. Laura was right. She'd tell lies!

THREE

While Ziggy lay at home worrying about how his sisters were in Liverpool, and while Julia had tea and toast with Laura and worried about her father, Luke 'Gonch' Gardner was making his way home and worrying about his Walkman.

'It was your own fault,' declared Gonch's friend, Paul 'Hollo' Holloway. 'You shouldn't have had it on in class.'

Gonch knew Hollo was right. He knew he was right because he had had his Walkman confiscated once before – which was why he was so worried now. It wasn't because he had been caught and received detention. For Gonch, detention was seen as almost a part of the school day. He could cope with that. What he couldn't cope with would be his mum's verbals when she discovered the Walkman was missing.

Gonch was definitely worried because his mum would definitely ask to see it when he got home. She always did. She always had. Ever since he had it confiscated last time. Now, every time he took it to school he had to show it to her when he came home. It was like being back in the infants!

Gonch remembered having to go through the same routine all through his very first school. It started when he started to take his Star Wars figures with him. He could never make his mum understand that everybody did. Everybody lent their toys to each

20

other. It was a way of making friends. However, it wasn't the lending his mum objected to, it was the swops. Everyone else seemed to put up with it – except his mum. Mind you, even Gonch could now see that five Space Troopers and a Darth Varder was too much for R2D2. He accepted that he had been swindled, but he only needed R2D2 at the time and he had tons of Space Troopers and three Darth Varders. Still, Tub Wilson shouldn't have robbed me like that, Gonch thought, whenever he remembered the incident. Of course, Gonch's mum couldn't see what a bandit Tub Wilson was. According to her, he didn't rob Gonch, it was Gonch who was 'stupid enough to give his things away!' Ever since that fateful day two things changed in Gonch's life. The first was that his mum never trusted him taking things to school – even now. The second was that Gonch vowed never to be taken advantage of again – he had learnt his lesson well.

However, although he had changed accordingly, his mum's attitude remained exactly the same. As far as she was concerned the root of every problem or incident lay with Gonch. The last time his Walkman was confiscated it was stolen from the Staff Room, but, like the Tub Wilson swap, that was not the robber's fault – but Gonch's for taking it to school in the first place!

She's brilliant, me mum, thought Gonch as he and Hollo walked past the dead cat that had been lying in the subway under the main road for the past two weeks.

'I wonder when the council are going to move that thing?' Hollo asked as they passed the rotting carcass.

Gonch turned to look, then spoke, but it wasn't the response Hollo was expecting. 'I bet you, if a Jumbo jet fell out of the sky and on to me head, me mum'd say it was my own fault for standing there.'

'You what?' Hollo asked, mystified by the connection with the removal of the dead cat.

'Me mum. Blames me for everything.'

'Oh,' said Hollo, then added, 'but if a Jumbo did land on your head, you wouldn't be worrying about what your mum thought, would you?'

True enough, thought Gonch turning to look at the dead cat as they left the subway. 'Dead cats don't vote, do they?' he suggested.

'No. But people who have to step over them do, though, don't they?' Hollo countered.

'Yeah. But no one uses these subways, do they. So no one's going to step over it.'

'We do,' protested Hollo.

'But we're not old enough to vote, are we, duck brain. And when we are – we probably won't come down here,' Gonch countered as they walked up the ramp and climbed over the fence to take a short cut through the old-age-pensioners' flats.

Gonch took another look back at the subway and wondered why they bothered using it themselves. It was dark, filthy and it stank. It was safer than crossing the main road, although he didn't really see that as a big enough obstacle to warrant using the subway. It was probably because no one else used it. Yeah. We bravely go where no pedestrian had gone before. Us and the dead cat!

Wonder how it did die, Gonch thought, as he bunked Hollo up over the wall at the back of the flats, pulled himself up on the wall and walked along the top until they reached the telephone box on the corner. With the windows out it made a great ladder. They were as quick at fixing telephone boxes as they were at removing dead cats.

Probably got run over, he thought as he dropped the last few feet on to the pavement and set off across the road that led to his house.

The cat probably didn't know about using the subway. It probably never had to suffer that boring road safety bloke the council sent round the school every year. And where was the Green Cross Code Man? Gonch grinned as they approached his house. Obviously doesn't give a stuff for cats. Although, thought Gonch, perhaps the cat did know its Green Cross Code, and what the subway was for – but didn't want to use it because it stank! So it tried to cross the road and got run over. Serves it right then, Gonch chuckled, but then stopped as the thought brought him back to his Walkman and his mother, who would be waiting to see it less than ten paces from his present position.

'Where are you going?' Hollo asked, slightly puzzled as he saw Gonch spin on his heel and walk away from his house.

'Back to school,' Gonch replied.

'What?'

'Back to school!'

'What for!?' Hollo asked as he turned to catch up.

'To get my bloody Walkman back!'

'But ∴. . but how? It's locked in the Staffroom, dimple head.'

'I know that.'

'Then how are you going to get it?'

'Break in.'

23

'What!?' Hollo stopped dead in his tracks. Had he heard Gonch correctly? 'What!?' he called as Gonch started to climb the telephone box.

'You heard,' shouted Gonch, as he ran along the wall and dropped out of sight into the pensioners' flats.

Hollo hesitated for a moment. Gonch was going to break into the school. He had just heard him say it, but he didn't believe it. He turned and looked up and down the road. There was no one in sight. So no one else could have heard them. No one else would know. He moved toward the telephone box and started to climb, but hesitated once again as he reached the wall, where he could see Gonch going through the block of flats, across the garden and toward the fence by the subway. Would Gonch really break in to the school so he wouldn't have to face his mum about the missing Walkman? Hollo looked back toward Gonch's road. He knew Gonch's mum. Yes . . . yes . . . Gonch would do it. So would I if she was my mum, he thought, as he started to move along the top. And if Gonch is going to break in, Hollo thought as he lowered himself into the flats and took off after Gonch, yeah . . . if he is going to break in, I want to be there to see it!!!

FOUR

By now Mickey Mouse was dragging his damaged finger toward the six on the clock face to make the time nearly half past five. Ziggy was even more miserable than he had been earlier. He was still on his own. His mum had come home from the shops, but had gone out again. The woman from the next flat was expecting a baby and had rushed in to tell his mum it was on its way. Well, she hadn't really rushed in, it was more a sort of waddle. Like a penguin, Ziggy thought. The woman had three other kids. As far as Ziggy could make out the oldest, a boy named Robert, although his mates called him 'Tank', was about eight. He had two younger sisters; Rachel, who looked about five or six, and Rosaline, who looked as far as Ziggy could tell, about two.

The three R's, Ziggy chuckled to himself. Robert, Rachel and Rosaline. Either the woman had a thing about the letter 'R' or she didn't have much imagination. Especially as her second name was Reynolds!

Wonder what this next one'll be, thought Ziggy. If it's a boy it'll probably be called Richard. If it's a girl, Rebecca or Roxanne or Ruth. They were the only names he could think of beginning with 'R'. That's probably one of the reasons why little Robert calls himself Tank, thought Ziggy. Although it's probably got more to do with the way he charges about. Right head the ball he is. Ziggy laughed as he remembered the first time he had come into contact with young Tank. He had nearly run him over with his bike.

It was actually on the day they had moved down from Liverpool. Ziggy's dad had hired a van and they had moved their furniture themselves. It was while they were unloading and while Ziggy was carrying a box full of crockery that Tank decided to try and set a new world land speed record on his bike. He had come charging round the corner, head down and leaning over the handle bars to give him a more aerodynamic shape. He was either unable to see or just not looking but it was only the swift departure of a cocker spaniel that alerted Ziggy that danger was approaching. He never could figure out how he got out of Tank's way, but he remembered throwing the box of dishes and plates up into the air and almost leap-frogging over the speeding biker, before catching the box just before it hit the ground. The only thing that stopped him going after Tank to sort him out was the fact that Tank himself got such a fright that he braked too quickly and went flying over the handlebars, straight into the hedge that surrounded his own front garden.

Fortunately, for Tank, the hedge saved him from any serious damage and after a session with the TCP and Elastoplast he was back out on the streets helping Ziggy and his dad carry the furniture into the house. Although he meant well, they teased him later that his help added about one and a half hours on to the job.

Still, Ziggy liked Tank. He was a bit like himself. The two of them suffered from the same problem. Trouble followed them around. Ziggy also liked the other two 'R's, Rachel and Rosaline, as it reminded him a bit of the way he, Michelle and Allison had been as kids. That was why he didn't mind his mum going in to look after the three R's, while their mum went off to hospital to produce a fourth. They didn't seem to have a dad, at least Ziggy had never seen him. One must exist somewhere though, thought Ziggy, or how else would there be another R on its way? Must be away a lot. Might be like us. Split up because the dad was unable to get work. Should be able to down south though. Not like it is up north. At least it isn't according to Dad, or why else would we be down here and Allison and Michelle be back in Liverpool?

Now that his thoughts had gone back to Liverpool he became more depressed. More so as his thoughts about the Reynolds family had reminded him so much of how things had been for him and his own family in the past, before his dad lost his job when his biscuit factory closed down.

Ziggy's mum had worked there for a time as well, as a part-time worker packing the biscuits into boxes. She used to be able to buy boxes of broken biscuits really cheap. It was great, that, Ziggy remembered. Every Thursday night when she came home, he and the girls used to dive in.

Our Michelle was a right pig then. Always shoved me aside until she could rummage through and grab all the chocolate ones. Our Allie was as bad, Ziggy chuckled, until I started going up to meet me ma at the bus stop. Had 'em all whizzed before we got home. Wish everything was still like that now.

Wonder what the girls are doing now, he thought as he eased himself out of bed and went across the landing to the toilet again. He didn't really want to go, but at least it was something to do.

27

He was on his way back to his room when his mum popped back in from next door.

'Eric! What were you doing in there?' Mrs Greaves asked suspiciously.

'What do you think I was doing?' replied Ziggy.

'I meant what are you doing out of bed?'

'I'm not a kid anymore, Ma. I gave up wetting the bed years ago, Ma. Remember?'

Mrs Greaves still eyed him with some suspicion but finally decided that her son, like everyone else, was entitled to use the toilet. Why are mothers so suspicious? thought Ziggy as he leaned against the bannister. He decided to take her mind off him by asking how things were next door.

'Not too bad,' replied his mum. 'But Mrs Reynolds' sister can't come across to look after the children until tomorrow.'

'Why not? She must have known about it.'

'Yes, but they didn't expect it until next week. So I said I'd look after the children until tomorrow.'

'Ah hey, Ma. We don't have to have flippin' Tank in here do we?'

'I might be soft-hearted, Eric, but I'm not soft in the head. Yet. I'm going to sleep next door.'

'And what about me?'

'You'll be all right. You're not a lad anymore – as you've just informed me.'

With that she moved off toward the kitchen. 'Do you want some tea?'

'Yeah. What's going?'

'Sausage, egg and chips.'

'OK!' he called and went back toward his bedroom. At least that's not too bad, he thought. Me favourite tea. Suppose it's quick and easy for me ma too. Hasn't had to look after three young kids for ages.

As Ziggy went back into the bedroom his eyes settled on the photo of him and his sisters. Michelle loved chips. But Allison became a food freak when she went into the sixth form. All brown bread and low fat diets. Looked good on it though, admitted Ziggy to himself. She's lost all those spots she used to have. He laughed. Must have given them all to our Michelle. He really missed the girls. He put the photo down and found himself rummaging amongst the rubbish he called possessions until he found an old train timetable to Liverpool. He started to look up the train as he heard his mum come into the room.

'Eric. I'm going back next door. I can't leave those children alone too long. As you're up and about now. . . .'

'I've only been the bog,' protested Ziggy.

'Never mind,' his mother continued, ignoring the protest. 'As you can get about a bit can you come and get your tea if I knock on the wall when it's ready?'

'Yeah . . . all right.' Ziggy agreed because he knew his mum too well. Especially that tone in her voice. Her 'or else' tone. He also knew she couldn't leave the Reynolds' children too long, especially if she was cooking.

His mum then leaned forward and kissed him on the forehead. 'OK . . . I'll see you later.'

As soon as she'd gone, Ziggy wiped his forehead and sat on the edge of the bed. If he was going to have to go next door and get his tea he didn't fancy lowering himself on to his back and then having to painfully manoeuvre himself out of bed again.

He looked at the timetable, and then at Mickey Mouse's hands. The next train was in two hours. I could get that if I wanted, Ziggy thought. And I'd still have time to get me tea. Once I've done that I wouldn't see me mum again till tomorrow, would I?

He turned the timetable over and looked at the times of the trains back from Liverpool. The earliest proper train got back at half past nine. That's no good, thought Ziggy. Mum would have taken those kids to school and dad would be back from work by then. He consulted the timetable again to discover there was an overnight sleeper that left Liverpool about midnight that would get him back at about five o'clock. I could be back home and in bed before half-seven with a bit of luck. He consulted the timetable again. If I made the next one tonight, I could be home by ten o'clock. See the girls. Bomb back to Lime Street and catch that sleeper train and be back here before me ma and da ever knew I was gone.

His mind began to race with the excitement of it all. He didn't fancy being on his own all night. He didn't fancy going to sleep next door. He'd love to see the girls again. His mum and dad wouldn't miss him until the morning. The girls wouldn't say anything, would they. Our Michelle might, he thought. Nah. Me and our Allie can talk her out of it.

He looked across at Mickey Mouse. There was time. If the sausage and chips didn't take much longer. There was a knock on the wall. It was ready. He looked at the timetable again. Was he being totally crazy? His back still stung like mad when he leaned against anything. His mum could pop back any minute during the night. Supposing his dad came home early? Nah, he muttered to himself. Why should he. I'll tell me ma not to bother about me. To look after the kids. Yeah – that'll keep her next door. Should I do it then? Yeah, he nodded his head. Yeah. Why not. It'll be a laugh, won't it. With a grin he stood up and went to get his sausages and chips.

Ziggy filled his stomach. Emptied the old coca-cola tin that acted as his piggy bank. Coated a bandage in the cream the doctor had given him for his back. Wrapped it around himself and pulled on his old Liverpool FC football shirt. It was actually too small for him now. His mum said he had grown out of it. He thought she had shrunk it in the wash. However, it was now too tight, but perfect to hold the bandage and cream against his body. On top of that he pulled a sweatshirt and wriggled inside his jeans. He dug out his trainers and his bomber jacket. Found the spare set of house keys and set off.

He felt a bit strange as he stepped out into the night. Not just because this was the first time he had been properly dressed for days, but also because of what he was attempting to do. He was half-way down the street when he stopped. What if me ma does pop in to see if I'm all right. He looked back at the house. Christ! I've forgotten to leave the light on.

He turned and hurried back. Every step brought a new fear. An increased doubt. God. What happens if she looks out the window? What happens if da's factory goes on strike? What'll happen if Tank throws one of his paddy fits? What if she does pop in? What if . . .? What if . . .? What if . . .?

There were a thousand 'what ifs', by the time he reached his bedroom and switched on the light. In so doing he added one more. If I put the light on now, I can't put it off. What if she notices and comes to switch it off. Hang on, hang on. He told himself. She'd only think I'd fallen asleep with the light on. That's no big deal. What about all the other things though. Anyone could blow the whole thing. Then what'd happen. She'd go bananas if she came back and saw I was missing. She'd really tear into me then, wouldn't she. At least she would when she found me.

Then the thought suddenly struck him. God, she wouldn't know where I was. She'd really panic, wouldn't she. He stood in the middle of his room and began to realise that the whole idea was ridiculous. A complete flight of fancy. A daydream. He was just beginning to accept the fact that it was both a silly and impossible thing to do, when another thought hit him. I'll leave her a note. Just in case. So if she does come back, at least she'll know where I am. Yeah. That'll stop her panicking.

Within two minutes he had scribbled: 'Dear Ma, feeling really homesick. Gone to see Michelle and Allison. Be back in the morning. Don't worry. Eric.' and was out of the house, down the road and heading for the tube. The incredible journey had begun.

FIVE

'The Library!' Laura suddenly shouted.

'What!?' Julia asked as she finally gave up the struggle to force her head through what was supposed to be the neck of her old red sweater.

'Tell your dad we're going to the Library.'

'Oh –' Julia pulled off the sweater and threw it on to the bed. The sweater had shrunk. Her mother had ruined another one. The third in the past six months. I do wish she'd read the instructions for that new washing machine, she thought. I'll run out of clothes soon.

She moved over to the wardrobe to see if there was anything else suitable to wear to a Jumble Sale. 'And why the Library?' she asked Laura.

Laura rolled her eyes in the way that told Julia she was being an absolute duck brain! 'When was the last time you saw any boys in the Library?'

Julia thought hard. She couldn't really remember. 'Yes. You're right,' she announced. To which Laura just rolled her eyes again. Of course she was right. She always was. Well. Almost. The last time Julia could remember seeing any boys in the Library was when those three boys from the Roscoe Mount private school were thrown out for making too much noise while looking at the pictures in the medical books. Boys could be so stupid at times. She reached for the yellow shirt she had bought with the money her Auntie Joan had given her last birthday. She liked Auntie Joan. She always smelled nice. Then another thought occurred to her. 'You know boys don't go to the Library. I know boys don't go to the Library. But does Dad know?'

'Perhaps not,' replied Laura. 'But I'll bet he'll accept that much easier than if you tell him boys don't go to Jumble Sales.'

Laura had a point, thought Julia. Again! And we'll soon find out if she is right – again! That sounds like Dad's car.

She moved to the window and sure enough her father's car was beginning the nightly ritual of squeezing through the iron gates of the driveway to the garage. Julia stood and watched for a moment. Stop on the far side of the road. Get out. Lock the car. Cross the road. Open the gates. Check there was no rubbish or sharp objects on the driveway, pavement or gutter that could damage the tyres. Back to the car. Unlock it. Get in. Drive across road. Stop. Reverse back across road to line up car with gates. Back again. Misjudge it again. Reverse. Stop. Drive in. He always misjudged it. Julia couldn't understand it. Years he'd been doing it. But he still couldn't get it right. She remembered how when they first moved to this house her mother used to go out each night to open and close the gates for him. But she soon got fed up with the ritual. Especially in the winter.

'God, does he always drive like that?' Laura's voice suddenly penetrated Julia's thoughts. She turned to see Laura leaning against the window frame. She had obviously come to see what was holding Julia's interest.

'Afraid so,' replied Julia as she turned back to finish dressing.

'I know how we'll get him to accept the Library

34

story, now,' giggled Laura.

'How?' Julia had to ask even though she could tell the answer was going to be silly.

It was.

'We could say we're going to get him a book called 'How to Drive through Narrow Gates!'

'That's almost as funny as a bowl of custard,' replied Julia, as she heard those same narrow gates being clanked shut outside. Her father would come in any second now. 'So what are we going to say?'

'We're . . . we're going because . . . I know, because we need to do some research for our school project,' offered Laura.

'On what?'

'Er . . . I don't know.'

'Great. He's bound to ask, you know.'

'Well . . . what about . . .' She looked around the room for inspiration. It came from Julia's shrunken sweater. Then she giggled. 'Clothes that don't shrink?'

'Oh, come on . . .' pleaded Julia. 'If we're going to lie it's got to be convincing. Teachers never give things such simple titles, do they.'

'That's true,' replied Laura. 'All right, then . . . er . . . what's it made of? They usually take some boring idea like that, don't they?'

Julia snatched up the sweater as she heard the front door open and close. He was in. She struggled to find the label, now lost in the tangle left after she pulled it off her head. It had to be there somewhere. 'I'm sure this only had two arms when I was trying to get it on a few minutes ago. Ah, here it is.' She looked. '20% wool and 80% Polywolythingemyjigwhatsit!' she announced.

35

'Man-made fibres!' declared Laura, then giggled again.

'What's funny now!' Julia demanded. She could feel the back of her neck tingle at the prospect of facing her father.

'God made Heaven and Earth. But Man made fibres!'

'What!?'

'It's a joke . . . oh forget it.'

'Laura, I'm not in the mood for that sort of joke.' She heard her father downstairs. He was obviously talking to her mother in the kitchen.

'All right, then.' Laura became serious as she could see the worried look on Julia's face. 'Although I still think all this is ridiculous about going to a Jumble Sale.'

'So you've said. So perhaps we should just forget the whole thing.'

'Oh come on . . . it's only a bit of fun. You're not doing anything really bad are you? He only thinks you're off running around with all kinds of boys. We know you're not, don't we?'

Julia nodded. She knew the point was not about going to the Jumble Sale or not, but about the way her father still treated her as a child. It wasn't fair. Just because he was . . . was . . . oh, what was that word her mother had used when Julia had complained to her last week. It reminded her of idiot. Idiosyncratic her mother had said. It meant he had a tendency for odd or strange behaviour. Perhaps Laura was right. Perhaps the right word was idiot!

Suddenly there was a loud knock on the bedroom door and Julia was snapped out of her thoughts. Then her father's voice. 'Julia! Are you decent?'

'Er . . . er. . . .' She looked to Laura for help. But Laura was also in a state of shock. Neither of them had expected the confrontation so soon. 'Er . . . yes, Dad,' she heard herself say automatically. God, the door was opening and they hadn't had a chance to think out their story properly. Never mind rehearse it.

'Oh . . . hello, Laura,' Julia's father said as he entered. Noticing Laura sitting on the bed, he also noticed, although he didn't comment, how tightly she was squeezing Julia's man-made red sweater. Julia then felt as though an electric shock had gone down her spine when her father next spoke. 'Have you anything planned for this evening?' he asked.

Julia threw another look to Laura. Does he know? How could he? What should I say? 'Er . . . er . . . why?' she finally stammered.

Mr Glover sighed. 'Julia. How many times must I tell you not to answer a question with a question.'

'Sorry.'

'Well?'

'Er . . . well. . . .'

'We're going to the Library, Mr Glover,' Laura piped up.

'Oh?' He turned to look at Julia.

'Er . . . yes. It's for our school project, Dad.'

'Is it. What's the topic?'

I knew it. I knew he'd ask. He always does, Julia groaned to herself. Now we've had it. Now he'll trip us up and go bananas about lying to him. Oh . . . why did I listen to Laura. I should have just – but her thoughts died away as she found herself once again listening to Laura.

'It's about textiles, Mr Glover,' Laura said with so

37

much confidence that Julia almost started to believe her as she continued. 'Man-made Fibres in our Modern Society,' she said, holding up the red sweater as evidence.

'Oh . . .' Mr Glover nodded, as he took the sweater from Laura and examined it. Julia could feel the sweat forming on her hands. He doesn't believe us.

But she didn't believe his next comment.

'Sounds interesting.' He turned to Julia and winked. 'You should speak to your mother, though. About how long man-made fibres last in her new washing machine. What time will you be back?'

This is it, thought Julia. This is it. This is where he catches us out. Still, they'd gone this far. 'When the Library closes, I suppose.'

'What time is that?'

Julia couldn't remember. She looked to Laura.

'Er . . . about 8.30, I think.'

Mr Glover nodded. 'No later than a quarter to nine back here, then. Understand?'

'Er . . . yes . . . fine,' Julia readily agreed.

She couldn't believe it. Mr Glover turned toward the door, but was stopped by Julia's curiosity. 'Why did you ask about tonight?'

'Oh, your mother is going over to your Auntie Joan's and I'm going to a School Governors meeting. Just wanted to make sure you were all right. Your dinner will be ready shortly. Are you eating with us, Laura?'

'Er . . . yes, thank you, Mr Glover.'

Julia's father nodded and then left. Julia waited for the door to close and then turned and gave Laura a hug, more from relief than anything else.

'That was a great title. How did you think of that?'

38

she asked. 'It's exactly the sort of thing old Thomas in Chemistry would come out with!'

Laura nodded, adopting the tone of false modesty. 'You see, it can be handy having a mum as a teacher. I know exactly the sort of rubbish they spout!'

The two girls were still giggling and beginning to plan their illicit evening out, when a knock on the door announced the return of Mr Glover and the shattering of their excitement. 'I've got to pass the Library on my way home. I'll pick you up. About 8.30?'

Julia nodded and slowly sank on to the bed as her father left, closing the door behind him. The two girls looked at each other. Damn!

SIX

While Laura and Julie made their way to the Jumble Sale, and Gonch and Hollo made their way back to Grange Hill, Ziggy stood in the middle of the huge hall at Euston Station. People kept knocking into him as he stared up at the huge noticeboard that gave all the details about the comings and goings of all the trains. It took him a couple of minutes to locate the Liverpool train. Departing from Platform 12 in five minutes. Ziggy felt a flutter in his throat. Five minutes. Flippin' eck! What am I going to do now, he thought as he found himself slowly walking toward Platform 12. How am I going to get on the flippin' train without a ticket?

Ziggy had had no trouble getting from his home to the station. He had had no trouble because he had decided to pay the fare. He had reasoned that it was best not to risk any aggro on the way out. He'd have enough of that when he got to Liverpool. The real problem he had now was that he didn't have enough money for the fare.

When he had emptied his coke tin he had thought he had had more than enough. It was only when he reached the plate glass screen of the ticket counter that he realised he didn't even have enough to buy a one-way ticket. He couldn't understand it. He remembered exactly how much his dad had paid when he came down for the interview for the job. He had tried to argue with the bloke behind the glass screen, but got nowhere. Ziggy had told him how much his dad had paid and the glass screen had told him that that had been a special excursion fare. It was only available from Liverpool to London, not from London to Liverpool. 'Why's that?' Ziggy had asked indignantly. It just didn't seem fair.

'Everyone wants to come to London, son. No one wants to go to Liverpool, do they?' the glass screen replied.

'I do!' said Ziggy.

'Then you'll have to pay the ordinary fare. If you haven't got enough money, go home. There's a queue behind you who do have the right money.'

Ziggy had turned to see a very agitated-looking man waving a credit card in his hand. As he walked away Ziggy couldn't help but wonder if the man had enough money, or whether he was getting into debt on his credit card. Even if he was the glass screen wouldn't care. And the man would get on the train. But how am I going to do it, Ziggy wondered as he walked toward the ticket barrier and watched the last few passengers shuffle their suitcases and bags toward the barrier. Only two minutes to go before the train was due to leave.

Ziggy's eyes scanned the station. He took in the row of telephone boxes, the book-stand, the chemist's shop, the bar, the cafe, but nowhere could he find an answer. All the entrances to the other platforms were either closed with shuttered gates, or had a ticket collector on duty. His eyes did another circuit of the station. Still no inspiration, until he spotted a platform ticket machine.

Ziggy immediately dashed toward the machine, pulling out the loose change in his pocket. He was

41

still about five metres from the machine when his hand froze in his pocket. Empty. The machine was empty. He looked around again. He was about to go and ask the ticket collector where he could buy a ticket when he spotted another form of platform ticket. Coming across the station toward him, well, not toward him but toward Platform 12, was a woman about the same age as his mum. But what was more interesting was the two suitcases, two carrier bags, the baby in the pushchair and the two year old toddler she was trying to steer toward the platform barrier.

Ziggy pondered for a moment, then acted on instinct. He dashed across to her, just as one of the carrier bags split and the toddler decided to go and have a look at the book-stall. 'You going to Liverpool, missus?' he asked.

'Er . . . yeah.'

'Carry your case for you if you like,' Ziggy offered.

'Er . . . OK.' The woman replied as she dumped the two cases and took off after her wandering child.

Ziggy grinned to himself. Great. I'll nip through the barrier pretending she's me mum. 'I'll take it over to the platform for you,' Ziggy called as he struggled toward the barrier with the bulging suitcase. What's she got in here, he wondered, but didn't spend too much time thinking about it as his brain was now tuning up to tackle the ticket collector. I'll try bombing straight past first, see how that goes, thought Ziggy, as he reached the barrier. It didn't 'go' very far.

'Where's your ticket, sonny?' the voice of the ticket collector boomed down.

'Er . . . me ma's got it!' Ziggy offered turning to look at the woman who, having recaptured her wondering toddler, was now heading toward the barrier. That should be enough for him, Ziggy thought as he turned to move away. It wasn't. He felt a heavy hand on his collar.

'Then why don't you wait for her?' boomed the ticket collector.

'I wanta to get a good seat,' Ziggy offered.

'They're all good seats,' countered the ticket collector as he punched two tickets belonging to the man with the credit card Ziggy had seen at the ticket counter. The woman now arrived at the barrier. 'This your boy?' the ticket collector asked.

'No, he just offered to carry me suitcase,' replied the woman, wondering what was going on.

'Didn't think he was.' He handed back the woman's tickets. 'You'd better hurry up, love. You've only got about thirty seconds.' The woman nodded, gathered up her bags, suitcase and children and staggered off toward the train. The ticket collector turned back to Ziggy. 'And you. You've only got about thirty seconds to disappear out of my sight.'

'I didn't say she was me ma, did I?' Ziggy protested, almost in desperation. Thirty seconds before the train goes.

'Didn't you?'

'No. You assumed she was.'

'Because you looked at her when you said it.'

'Yeah . . . because I was helping her to carry her cases, wasn't I? Me real ma's on the train, isn't she?'

'Is she?'

'Of course she is.'

'Can't be much of a mother then, can she?'

'You what?!' Ziggy asked, totally mystified by this assumption.

'Well,' said the ticket collector as he nodded toward

43

the clock and then at the guard about to wave his flag for the train to depart. 'That train will be gone in about fifteen seconds and I can't see any signs of your mother looking worried about where you've got to. Can you?'

Ziggy was caught out. He knew it. He realised the guy must have seen him hanging about outside. What should I do, he thought. Leg it for the train? Nah. He'd have me, wouldn't he. Or he'd shout to his mates down there. He decided to have one last try. 'She hasn't got a watch. She mightn't know it's about to go!'

'Then what would she think we go along closing all the doors for?'

Ziggy gave up. He knew he'd never get past this guy. He also knew it was too late. He heard the guard's whistle blow, and saw the train start to move slowly along the platform. He stood staring. Watching it crawl its way along the platform and out of the station. He hardly heard the ticket collector's voice as he started to close the shuttered gates across the barrier.

'Never mind, son. Perhaps you're mum'll send you a postcard!'

Ziggy only stopped staring after the train when his view was blocked by the gate clanking shut. He stood for a moment wondering what to do next before he turned away. His dream was shattered. The incredible journey had come to an end. Before it had even started!

SEVEN

Ziggy's incredible journey may have ended before it started, but for Gonch and Hollo theirs was about to begin.

'Hasn't he got a home to go to?' Gonch groaned as he slid down the wall behind the kitchen dustbins.

'You'd think this *was* his home, the way he carries on,' Hollo replied as he flicked a small pebble toward an empty crisp packet lying on the grass in front of them. He was trying to see if he could flick a pebble into it. He had been trying for half an hour while they waited for Mr Griffiths, the school caretaker to disappear for the night. Hollo must have flicked at least a hundred pebbles, but he hadn't got one in yet.

'Yeah,' said Gonch. 'Remember when he nearly caught me squirting water over Fuzzy Benson? I thought his hair was going to blow off the top of his head.'

'It would have done if he had caught you.'

'No way,' countered Gonch, but then added, 'it'd have been my hair that got separated from my head – not his.' Then he laughed. 'What did he say? "Drips. Drips like messing about with water!"'

Hollo now laughed. 'Remember that time he did catch us swinging on the door to the Assembly Hall?!' Hollo then took on a voice that was supposed to sound like Griffiths but sounded more like that actor on the telly who always plays Sergeant-Majors in comedy programmes. 'How long do you think that door will last if you 'orrible little lot keep swinging on it? Doors are made to open and close, not carry passengers. Now – hop it!'

Gonch just grinned. He remembered that incident. And remembered how Griffith's words had become a catch-phrase. They had all gone round for weeks saying, 'How long do you think such-and-such will last if you lot keep using it?!' In the end it had got to the point when no one could do anything without someone saying, 'How long do you think that would last. . . .' Gonch even remembered catching Hollo with, 'How long do you think your nose will last if you keep picking it? Noses are made for breathing in and out of, lad. Not for picking!'

'What are you grinning about?' Hollo asked.

'Just Griffiths,' replied Gonch. He then edged himself up to look over the wall once again.

'See anything?' Hollo said, then tutted. Not at Gonch or what he could or couldn't see. But because he nearly got a pebble into the crisp packet.

'No,' replied Gonch. 'Looks all quiet now.'

'You going to risk it?'

'Not yet,' Gonch said as he slid back down the wall once again. 'We'll wait a bit longer. In case he comes back.'

'Are you sure about this, Gonch? I think it's crazy.'

'You don't have to be here.'

'I know, but. . . .' Hollo's voice tailed off. The thought remained unstated. It didn't matter. Gonch knew what he was thinking. They were mates. Good mates. They shared everything and looked after each other. They always had since they met in the Infants.

46

Gonch looked at Hollo. Another pebble missed. What a lousy shot, thought Gonch. He is a good mate, though. And I suppose I'm being a bit unfair. It's not his mum that's a bleedin' nuisance, is it?

'Look, Hollo . . .' Gonch spoke. 'Er . . . you don't have to be here. Honest. I can do this by myself, you know.'

Hollo knew what his friend was thinking. That there was no need for them both to get into trouble. But he knew that Gonch would welcome the support. They had been through a lot together. A lot of trouble and a lot of fun. He knew it wasn't really his worry. It wasn't his mum. But it was his friend. And his friend's problems became his problems. He thought all this but said to Gonch 'I know you can. But it won't be half as much fun without me, will it?'

That was true. Gonch laughed and took another look over the wall of the bin store. Still no sign of Griffiths. He stooped back down again. 'All quiet,' he said to Hollo. 'We'll give it a bit longer before we go.'

Hollo nodded. Flicked another pebble. Missed again. 'What do you think makes Griffiths like he is?' he asked Gonch.

'Dunno. Loves this place though, doesn't he?'

'Yeah,' Hollo nodded. 'Probably because he doesn't have to come here. He's not forced to, is he? He took the job, didn't he?'

'Yeah. But perhaps he didn't have much choice. It's not easy finding jobs these days. Look at that new bloke, Ziggy Greaves. His dad had to move down from Liverpool to find a job.'

'Yeah. Well. Who cares. Griffiths is a pain in the bum. And he's here. And we have to put up with him. Blast!' Hollo had hit the side of the crisp packet but the pebble had bounced out.

Gonch just smiled. That's the only trouble with Hollo, he thought. He doesn't really think too much. Something happens because it happens. Might be the best way really. Makes life much simpler.

He sat with his thoughts for a moment, and decided that he personally thought too much. He always wanted to know about everything. Not necessarily his school work. Most of that he found easy. It was just boring. No, what Gonch was always curious about was why people did what they did. Where did they come from? Where does that road go to? What's behind that door? Hollo reckoned he'd make a great copper one day. Gonch preferred to think along the lines of Special Investigator. Naturally curious was how he described himself. Bloomin' nosey parker was how Hollo described him.

As he let his thoughts drift, Gonch accepted that half the reason behind breaking into the school was just to see what it would be like after hours. He'd always tried to imagine it: quiet; echoing; hushed silence. Spooky, probably. It was hard to believe with twelve hundred screaming pupils charging back and forth. Gonch was sure it took hours for the noise to die away, like it took hours for the swimming baths to become still after everyone had got out for the day. He had always wanted to know. Now he was about to find out. However, as he stood up to take another look over the wall he also had to admit it wasn't just natural curiosity that drove him on. It was the natural fear of his mum if he came home without his Walkman.

It was all clear.

'Right,' said Gonch, as he tapped Hollo on the

shoulder. 'Come on.'

The two mates hesitated for a moment. Then Hollo got to his feet. Gonch led the way toward the end of the bin store wall, but stopped for another quick look around. They had already decided that they would make a dash across the playground and try to get in through the boiler room. Through Mr Griffiths' own boiler room.

It had been Gonch's idea. While they were waiting for old Griffiths to lock up they had realised that every door and window would be secured. After all, Griffiths wouldn't leave the school open for burglers, would he? Hollo had suggested trying the roof, to see if there were any skylights they could get through. Gonch wasn't too keen. He thought they'd be too noticeable. He didn't fancy risking the climb and he certainly didn't fancy dropping through the roof into the school. What about getting out? Even Hollo had accepted that was too much of a risk.

It was probably Gonch's worry about being seen on the roof that made him think of going in underground. Whatever it was, he had suddenly remembered the time the school witch, Imelda Davis, and her gang had shoved a first-year girl down an old disused coal chute into the boiler room. Gonch had heard talk of them having it sealed off after this incident, but he couldn't remember ever seeing it done. That's how they would get into the school building. Once inside he was sure there was some underground ducting that took all the heating pipes round to the school. He was also sure there were manholes in each corridor so they could repair and maintain the system. That was how they would get inside the school itself.

'Let's go,' Gonch said to Hollo, but as they went to move, Gonch suddenly stopped. 'Just want to try something,' he said.

'What?' Hollo asked as he saw his friend bend down to pick up a pebble. Then saw him flick it at the crisp packet. It went straight in. Gonch laughed and dashed out from behind the wall and across the playground. The swine, thought Hollo, but turned and followed his friend.

By the time Hollo reached Gonch, he had already located the entrance to the coal chute. Not only that, but he was already using an old chair leg to prise away at the padlock that locked it.

'You'll never get that off,' Hollo protested. But even as he said it he knew he was wrong. He had seen Gonch in this mood too often. Sure enough, the lock came off with a sharp crack. The noise was so loud that Hollo was sure every resident in every street around Grange Hill had heard it. Any second, armies of people would come running round the side of the school building. Hollo suddenly felt very exposed crouching next to the boiler house. He felt very alone and he was: Gonch was gone. Then he heard his voice.

'Come on, then.'

Hollo looked into the chute – it was pitch black.

'Come on,' Gonch urged. 'And pull the door closed after you!'

Hollo took one last look round. To his amazement everything was still quiet. With a deep breath he took hold of the door and pulled it closed behind him. He slid down the chute. The moles of Grange Hill were loose.

EIGHT

While Gonch and Hollo were starting their underground journey, someone else was back underground as well. Ziggy was on the tube train on his way home.

He was slumped forward, his elbows resting on his knees, rocking from side to side between the stiff armrests that divided up the seats. He was fed-up and miserable. He had thought about trying to get on the next train to Liverpool but had worked out that it wouldn't arrive until nearly eleven o'clock. By the time he'd travelled from Lime Street Station to his Auntie Ann's it would be time to get the overnight train that would have him home and in bed before his mum discovered he was missing. There was nothing for it now but to go back.

I must have been stupid anyway, he thought. I mean, what a divvy. Thinking I could make it up there and back anyway without me ma finding out. You're a right bone brain, Ziggy, me old son. A right bone brain.

He glanced up at the Underground diagram on the wall of the carriage. Four more stations before his. He would get off the train there and go home to face whatever was coming. And knowing his mum, he knew it would mean the back of her hand. His dad never hit him, but his mum did. Only once or twice, but it was enough. She packed quite a punch.

God, she'll be furious, thought Ziggy. Remember

that time I went missing at the fair. Crazy she was. Really crazy. Told me she'd been worried out of her mind. Imagined all sorts had happened to me. So what does she do when she sees me – smack. Back of her hand. Right round the lughole. Ziggy couldn't help but grin. Head-the-balls me ma and da. Like me da smacking our Allie one when she stayed out late with Dopey Dennis. Worried about us so – smack. He grinned again. I'm worried about you, so come here, I want to beat you up. Aaahh. . . . It's probably frustration at not being able to do nothing. Gets me like that sometimes. Aagghh . . . like now!

Ziggy's wince was caused by leaning back on the seat. Since leaving home he had not paid much attention to his still-injured back. Now, as the action of leaning back against the seat caused the itching and stinging to start once more, it was uppermost in his thoughts. Like that bloody Imelda, thought Ziggy as he slowly moved his shoulders up and down to ease the stinging. I really feel like giving her a good smack. Will and all when I get back to Grange Hill. She'll regret the day she stuffed fibreglass down my back.

The train stopped at a station. Three more to go before Ziggy's stop. Three people got on – two of the new arrivals were a couple of guys about the same age as himself. The only problem was that one of them was carrying a ghetto blaster. Worse than that. It was blasting out 'Wham!'

Ziggy couldn't stand 'Wham!' If he'd been in any better frame of mind he might even have considered changing carriages. However, in his present depressed state he merely glanced up at the route diagram to see how many more stations he would have to suffer George Michael.

As he turned his eyes away he was drawn once again to the poster next to the route diagram. The train with the front shaped like Concorde. It was an advert for people to take the tube train to Heathrow Airport. Ziggy looked back at the route diagram. The train he was on would actually go to the airport.

A strange thought was beginning to form in Ziggy's head. It was even wilder than his original idea. What about a plane? He racked his memory. Yeah . . . yeah . . . he remembered. The last plane to Liverpool was about eight o'clock. He remembered 'cos Uncle Jimmy and Auntie Doe had come back from holiday on it. It gets in about nine o'clock as well. Even earlier than the train. If I could get that I'd be well in to see the girls and get the overnight train. Ye-e-es.

His thoughts began to accelerate but were slowed down momentarily when 'Wham!' were suddenly stopped dead in their mid-tracks. The ghetto blaster carrier was rummaging in his pocket for more musical ammunition. Silence. Well, nearly silence except for the rattle and clatter of the train as it picked up speed out of the station. Next stop was Ziggy's.

The momentary silence had allowed Ziggy's thoughts to slow down and he began to think about the difficulties that lay ahead. If he didn't have enough money to pay for a train ticket, he definitely wouldn't have enough for a plane. So I'll have to sneak on, he decided. I got caught at the train because I wasn't expecting to have to sneak on. It was a last minute thing. That ticket bloke saw me hanging about. Hesitating and that. This time I'll be more prepared, won't I? Get there. Suss it out. Straight in. Look like I know what I'm doing.

He glanced up at the route diagram again.

Heathrow Airport was only a few stops after his own. I'd be well there by eight o'clock. Half-seven probably. Yeah. Half-seven he decided as he noticed a new cassette slide into the ghetto blaster. A hand moved toward the play button. God, I bet this'll be 'Bucks Fizz', looking at the state of those two. It wasn't. It was 'Relax' by Frankie. Ziggy couldn't believe it. It also made up Ziggy's mind as the train began to slow down for his station. It's an omen, he thought. Relax, don't do it! Dead right I will. I mean, me ma'll be ready to clock me one anyway. Just for trying to do it. So I might as well have a go, might'n I?

The train stopped. Another wave a doubt flowed over Ziggy. What if me ma has found I'm missing? What if she's phoned the police? Got me da home from work? What'll I do when I get to Liverpool? How can I sneak on a plane, anyway? They're always on the look out for terrorists and that, aren't they? Ohhh, it's stupid, this is. It'll never work. But why not? I read about those two kids who got across to New York from Manchester, didn't I? They were only sussed by a cop in New York City. It can be done. His thoughts began to race as he sensed the doors would soon close and the train leave his station. If . . . if me ma is in a state she'll survive for a few more hours, won't she? She did when I went missing all day at the fair. Anyway, I could phone up Auntie Ann from the airport. She'll know if the bubble's burst. If it has I can go home. If not. . . . But how am I going to get on the plane? They have got all kinds of security and that, haven't they? Yeah, but. . . . His thoughts were interrupted by the loud hiss and rumble that signalled the train doors were about to close. And they did. The train started to move again.

Ziggy grinned. Yeah, he thought, they do have all kinds of security, but terrorists still get through, don't they? And they won't be looking for a five foot twelve-year-old terrorist, will they? He glanced up at the route diagram once more, then down toward the ghetto blaster. Yeah, I'll have a crack, he thought. Frankie says – Relax! The incredible journey was back on.

NINE

Although Ziggy, Gonch and Hollo were all carrying on their various subterranean activities, Julia and Laura were carrying on much more normal activities above ground. While Ziggy was on his way through a railway tunnel to Heathrow Airport and Gonch and Hollo were about to tunnel their way beneath Grange Hill, the girls were doing nothing more exciting than handing over 50p to gain entrance to St Saviour's Grand Jumble Sale – all proceeds to go toward the new mini-bus. That's what the poster outside the Church Hall announced. Laura and Julie had no reason to dispute it.

St Saviour's was an independent school for autistic children and relied very much on voluntary donations and gifts to keep going. Every year they had a Jumble Sale and a Garden Fete. They always called them 'Grand' on all the posters and tickets and things; although Laura had never seen any reason why they should be called 'Grand', she had to admit it sounded better. She had first found out about these two annual events three years ago, and she'd been every year since.

'Why, though?' Julia asked as they walked into the Church Hall to see all the tables piled high with junk. 'Why do you come every year?'

Laura just shrugged. 'It's a worthwhile cause, I suppose. And if I'm going to waste my money on junk, I might as well waste it in a good cause.' Julia nodded, but then continued, 'How did you find out about it?'

56

'Dad. Being the magpie he is, he knows all the decent sales to come to. This is supposed to be good because everyone supports it.'

'They've certainly got a lot of stuff,' said Julia as she looked around the stalls.

'They made nearly a thousand pounds last year.'

'Wow!' Julia whistled. She could see why, though. The place was packed. A lot of money was changing hands.

'Let's go and have a look at the Victorian lace stall,' suggested Laura.

'Where is it?'

'I just saw it somewhere . . . oh . . . there. Over in that corner!' She pointed to the far corner and set off to fight her way through the crowd.

It would be, thought Julia, as she followed. She shouted to Laura. 'Don't forget! 8.30! We need to be at the Library.' She knew Laura and knew the reminder was necessary. Once she got involved in this, she'd be really difficult to get away. Although Julia didn't know it then, Laura would be more difficult than usual to get away tonight.

In fact it would be extremely difficult. It would also, for a change, not be her fault. It would have nothing to do with either of them, but with someone else who, unknown to Laura and Julia was just entering the Church Hall. If they had seen who it was, or if they had seen how they were getting into the Hall they might have guessed the night would end in trouble. As it was, they were both too busy fighting their way towards the Victorian lace to notice the new arrival was none other than the Grange Hill witch herself, Imelda Davis. She was entering by squeezing through the window in the Ladies' toilet. Anything to save 50p.

Still, despite the fact that wherever Imelda went, trouble was not too far behind, the first half-hour of the Jumble Sale went off without incident. It may have been because Imelda was not with her usual friends, Georgina Hayes and Helen Kelly, but with another girl and two boys, none of whom went to Grange Hill, but who lived near Imelda. However, though things remained peaceful early on, it was more than likely that Imelda was planning something.

She was.

At about halfpast seven, just as Ziggy Greaves was arriving at Heathrow, Imelda and her cronies were planning to make their move. They might have got away with it too, if it hadn't have been for Laura wanting to go to the loo!

Laura had left Julia rummaging through a pile of old sweaters as she fought her way through the crowd. Owww! She cursed to herself as someone stood on her toes, for about the hundredth time. She was glad she'd put her boots on. She'd be crippled by now in her trainers – another tip she had picked up from her dad.

Suddenly she felt herself standing on something soft. It moved. God, what's that, she thought, as she tried to look down through the seething crowd. She needn't have bothered. Its owner soon let her know what it was. 'Oh my God!' screamed a woman in a blue woollen coat. 'Oh my God! That's my foot you're standing on, if you don't mind!' The woman sounded both indignant and in pain.

'I'm terribly sorry,' offered Laura.

'So you should be ... oohh ... it's got to be broken. It's got to be.'

Laura could now look down. The woman had

created such a noise and such a fuss that even the throbbing mob of people had found some space to clear a patch. She sat on the edge of one of the stalls and started to massage the toes she claimed were broken. By this time Laura's sympathy was ebbing away. The woman was making too much fuss. She also should have known better than to wear open-toed shoes at a Jumble Sale. Laura decided she had had enough of her wingeing. 'I'm terribly sorry,' she said 'but it was an accident and I've had my own toes trodden on several times tonight. It's just one of those things.'

'It may be to you, young lady. But it's not your toe that's broken.'

'Oh don't be silly,' Laura said. She couldn't help it. 'If any of your toes were broken you wouldn't be able to massage them like that.' With that she turned and headed for the Ladies' toilet. God, she thought, as she pushed her way through the crowd. What a wally. She was almost as bad as Julia's father.

And it was this short incident that led, indirectly, to Julia's problems with her father. It was one link in the chain of events about to be started by Imelda and her cronies as they moved in on the raffle stall. This stall always took the most money, and tonight was no exception. Imelda and her cronies were planning to steal the raffle money!

The next link in this chain of events was the way, due to her bad temper, Laura closed the window in the Ladies' toilet – the same window Imelda had sneaked in through. However, Imelda would not be going out that way. Laura slammed the window shut with more force than she might normally have done. The result was that the handle broke in her hand –

and without the handle the window would be very difficult to open!

'Damn,' cursed Laura. 'That stupid woman!' She then went into the cubicle and slammed the door. Fortunately, the handle on that did not break.

Outside in the Hall itself, Julia was enjoying herself browsing among all the rubbish, although she was careful to keep one eye on her digital watch. 7.26. They would have to leave for the Library no later than eight o'clock. She moved on to a bric-a-brac stall and picked up a kind of musical box. It looked a bit like an old Japanese temple. If a button was pressed on the top, a tune was played and all the walls of the octagon opened to reveal small cup-like recepticles on the inside of each wall. Julia had noticed it when someone else was playing with it. She examined it and decided that at three pounds she would buy, found her purse and offered the money to the stall holder. 'Is it a jewellery box?' she enquired.

The stallholder laughed. 'No dear. It is, or it was, a cigarette box. The cigarettes stand inside those little cup things.'

'Oh,' said Julia, quite surprised. Like Laura she detested cigarettes and tobacco. Still, she liked the box. 'It *was* a cigarette box!' she said to the stallholder. 'Now, it *is* a jewellery box!' She exchanged a smile with the stallholder and turned away. As she did she saw Imelda Davis. And saw what she was doing. She had to look twice to make sure she believed what she was seeing. She looked twice. She believed it. Davis was stealing the raffle money.

As people came up and bought tickets for the Giant Teddy Bear, the money was dropped into a large biscuit tin behind the counter. Imelda Davis, shielded by her three cronies in crime, had straightened a metal coat hanger, hooked the biscuit tin and was pulling it toward her.

Julia looked around. What should she do? Who should she tell? Where was Laura? She then realised that there was no time to find any of the answers to these questions. She had to act. She did. 'Davis!' she yelled. No one seemed to notice. There was too much noise and confusion. 'Davis!!' she screamed. Still no response except for a few people near by who tut-tutted and shook their heads. 'Why can't young people learn some manners!' someone muttered.

Now Julia couldn't believe what she was seeing! She was screaming and no one was taking any notice. 'Hey! On the Raffle Stall. Hey! She's taking the money! Thief!! Look!! They're stealing the money!!!'

At long last people started to react to the words 'thief' and 'stealing', but everyone was confused. They could see Julia shouting. They could see her trying to push her way through the crowd. But they couldn't see why. They couldn't see Imelda. Some people thought it was Julia who was the thief.

'Not me,' she screamed. 'Over there. On the raffle.'

A few faces turned. It was enough to alert Imelda's cronies. Julia grew desperate. She could see them starting to get away. They were heading for the next link in the chain. The Ladies' toilet.

Laura was just coming out of the cubicle when Imelda came dashing in, closely followed by the girl and the two boys. She stopped dead in front of Laura, spilling money from the biscuit tin all over the floor. It wasn't Laura she was worried about, but the closed window. She then turned and rushed back outside.

Her cronies followed. Laura followed, totally bewildered by these events.

By the time Laura reached the toilet door, Imelda was leading her cronies out toward the main door, still clutching the biscuit tin full of money. Julia could see that unless she did something quickly they would get away. She looked around for inspiration. It came from the Bake'n'Bring Stall. Within a moment a huge trifle was flying toward Imelda. It hit her right between the shoulder blades. She was covered. So was everyone within a three metre radius. Including an even more bewildered Laura.

Still, the flying trifle had the desired effect. Imelda dropped the tin. The money scattered everywhere, and people rushed to save it.

'Why do people always go for money first?' groaned Julia. 'No,' she yelled. 'Get them first!' She pointed at Imelda and her cronies, now pushing their way out of the door, but everyone was too concerned about the cash. Julia was furious. She had done everything she could to stop it happening and they let them get away! She was even more furious a few moments later when the police arrived. They insisted she give a full statement. Not only would this delay them getting to the Library, it would mean her father was bound to find out what she had been up to tonight, and that she had lied to him.

Her anger turned to worry and then to incredulity. How can you get yourself into so much trouble trying to help somebody else?!

TEN

Ziggy had decided not to risk trying to get away without paying the excess fare for the extra ride he had taken on the tube train. He had worked out roughly how much it would be and that he would have enough to get back home if he couldn't get on to the plane.

He had had to work everything out between the last two stations before the airport. He had only had this length of time because the ghetto blaster had stayed on the train until then. The Frankie track had only been a momentary respite from all that 'Wham!' nonsense. Posey disco crap, was how Ziggy described it. Anyway, once Wham-head and his ghetto blaster had got off the train Ziggy had settled down to work out his plan of action. Even his back didn't hurt as he leaned back on the seat.

There's bound to be some kind of ticket bloke on the door, isn't there, Ziggy had pondered, thinking back to his experience at Euston Station. Heathrow Airport will be just like Euston only with planes instead of trains. What I'll have to figure out is how to get past that bloke, or get meself a ticket. Nah. No chance of that. You can't even fiddle the tube tickets. Or the bus. Never mind a flippin' plane. Nope. It's gonna have to be bunkin' in. But how? Ziggy had then worked out that there would probably be more than one guy to get past because of the higher security precautions at an airport. He was right. But he didn't realise how right he was until he got there.

His first experience was finding his way out of the tube station and into the right building to find the Liverpool plane. The first part was easy. He just followed the WAY OUT signs and paid his excess fare. The second part was a bit more difficult. As he came out into what looked like a huge underground tiled and marbled cavern, he was faced with a bewildering array of signs. 'WELCOME TO HEATHROW.' 'WAY OUT' 'TERMINAL 1' 'TERMINAL 2' 'TERMINAL 3' 'TERMINAL 4' Which way should he go? Which Terminal did he want? He looked round once more. Although he didn't want to attract attention to himself there was nothing for it. He would have to ask. 'Hey, mate,' he called to the train ticket collector. 'Where'd you get the Liverpool plane?'

'In Liverpool, I guess.' chuckled the ticket collector.

Ziggy rolled his eyes. Why does everyone have to be a comedian. 'I mean here, don't I.' He was going to add 'bubble brain' but decided against it. He wanted the answer more than he needed to score the point.

'Terminal 1. Follow the signs.'

Ziggy hurried away to follow them, throwing a 'Ta, mate,' over his shoulder.

The first place the signs took him was into one of the largest and biggest corridors he had ever seen. It must have been about ten metres across and about three metres high. There was a pathway down the middle, and on either side, against the walls, was a moving rubber walkway. You just stood on it and it moved along. A bit like a flattened out escalator, Ziggy thought as he looked up and down the corridor.

There was a funny pattern on the wall tiles and at first he couldn't make it out. He was too close to it on his own side, but looking across he realised it was a series of mosaics of different parts of the world. Well, at least that's what Ziggy reckoned as he passed. Could be some of the places you can fly to from London. Not bad that, he thought. He liked that idea, even if he was disappointed that he couldn't see anything to do with Liverpool anywhere.

Then he decided to run, partly to give him as much time as possible to suss out the ticket situation, but partly just to see what it was like to run along a moving walkway. It was great. As he ran his speed was automatically increased by the walkway and he felt himself almost rocketing along. As he ran faster the sensation increased. It was almost like being Superman, he thought, as he rocketed at superspeed past a young couple sitting on their suitcases. Ziggy looked over his shoulder. They looked knackered, as though they've been travelling for ever, he thought. But they had enough energy to laugh as Ziggy turned back to the front, just in time to see himself roaring down on another and older group of travellers and their suitcases, who were completely blocking the walkway.

Ziggy only had time to jump instinctively into the air over their suitcases. Things might not have been so bad if it had happened at the beginning or the middle of the walkway, but it hadn't. It had happened at the end. The result was that Ziggy took on another of Superman's super powers and flew through the air. Unfortunately that's where the similarity to 'Big S' ended. Still at superspeed, he came down with a terrific crash on the non-moving, non-rubber, tiled floor.

He landed hard on his knees, with such a thump he thought he'd loosened his fillings, and then he only had enough time to roll out of the way as the group of travellers and their suitcases were poured off the end of the still moving walkway.

The older group tut-tutted at his antics. They never even asked if he'd hurt himself. The younger couple were still laughing but did ask if he was all right. He nodded as he struggled to his feet and banged his aching knees – he didn't know why, but it seemed to ease the pain.

Ziggy then tried to run. He couldn't even walk. He leaned against the wall, his knees throbbing with pain. Bone brain. Divvy. Soft idiot. He cursed himself. Come 'ead, legs. You've got to get me upstairs. Come 'ead. Just get us up there and we'll suss it all out. Then you can have a rest.

His legs were obviously still on his side, or were becoming as embarrassed as the rest of Ziggy at the looks he was getting from other people passing. Whatever it was it worked. As he tried another step his right leg moved. Then the left. Slowly at first, but then increasing their pace as he followed the flow of people to Terminal 1. His legs were then delighted to find that they didn't have to go upstairs at all. They could use a lift. Ziggy followed a few people in and watched someone press the 'DEPARTURES' button.

As the lift doors opened, Ziggy experienced a strange sensation. He was facing the wrong way. He had not turned round. He had not moved. But he was facing the wrong way. The lift doors were open and everyone was beginning to move out, but Ziggy was still facing the way he came in. He had seen those doors close. They were still closed.

As he found himself being sucked out with the rest of the people he was beginning to wonder if the lift had turned round, when it dawned on him. It had two sets of doors! Divvy, he thought. Obvious. Must be the pain in me knees making me not think straight. Divvy.

With that problem solved Ziggy found himself following the rest of his fellow lift passengers into the terminal building itself. It was enormous. He had never seen a building so big. He was so overcome by it that he found himself slowing down to take it all in.

Wonder where you go to get on the planes, he wondered. Then he began to notice the number of television sets hanging from the ceiling or standing on pedestals. He took a closer look and realised they were like the video display units or VDU's they used on the school computers. They had rows and rows of numbers like BD92 1930 BOARD GATE 49; BA4532 2030 BOARD GATE 5. As he looked the screen suddenly changed and the numbers changed to BD92 1930 BELFAST; BA4532 2030 MANCHESTER. Ziggy scanned the display and found BD590 2010 LIVERPOOL. His heart jumped. That's it. He looked at the digital clock near the VDU's. 19.29. Plenty of time yet. But which airline? He looked round the terminal building hoping for a clue. He saw the shops. The cafe. The signs for the toilets. Even a sign for a bank. At this time of night, he wondered, but continued his visual search. He saw the telephones. But no clues as to what airline had BD590. However, the telephones reminded him of something else. He'd better phone Auntie Ann to see if the bubble had burst and his mum had the police out looking for him. No use carrying on if he was going to have to turn himself in at Heathrow, was there.

He wandered over to the telephones, arranged in small groups of four so they formed little islands. He found 10p, but then realised he'd probably need more to phone Liverpool. He selected a fifty pence piece as he picked up the receiver, but then stopped. He couldn't find anywhere to put the money. He looked again and realised he'd walked into a credit card phone. Plastic money again, he thought as he moved to the next one. He'd seen adverts for those phones but never actually seen one anywhere. Amazing place this, he thought, as he dropped in the fifty pence and the 'DIAL NOW' symbol came up on the phone. It made him hesitate. Was he doing the right thing? I don't normally phone Auntie Ann, he thought. What if she wonders what's going on and wants to check it with me ma? I'll be sussed then, won't – but he stopped in mid-thought. No I won't. She can't if we're not on the phone can she!! Right. I'll just say I want to speak to Allie about somethin', that's all. No harm in that, is there.

He started to dial. 051- for Liverpool. Then the number. There was no answer. His heart began to sink. There's no one in. There's no one in. He began to panic. What did that mean? Has me ma phoned? Are they all out looking for me? He forced his mind to slow down as the gentle burr-burr sounded in his ear. If me ma had put the bubble in someone would be waiting by the phone wouldn't they. For news and that. So, that means she hasn't. Everything's still OK at this end. Great. Ziggy began to calm down at this thought. He began to mutter. But where are they?

Come 'ead, Auntie. Answer the bloody phone.

Suddenly all his calm vanished as the continual burr-burr of the unanswered phone created another terrible thought in his head. What if they're not in? What if I manage to get up there, get to the house and find there is no one in? What do I do then? What – but his thought was interrupted by someone picking up the phone.

'Hello,' said a crackly voice. It also sounded out of breath.

'Hello. Auntie Ann?' Ziggy asked.

'Who's that?' demanded the voice, obviously now a bit annoyed at being disturbed.

'It's me. Eric, Auntie Ann.'

'Eric?'

'Yeah. Is Allie in?'

'You in London, Eric?'

'Er ... yeah,' Ziggy answered, but was on his guard. Was that a trick question? 'Yeah. Course I am.'

'You all right?'

'Yeah.' Was this another trick question? 'Course I am, why?'

'Just asking. Can ask after me own nephew, can't I?'

'Oh ... yeah.' Ziggy realised everything was OK. The bubble was still intact. 'Is Allie in?'

'No.'

Ziggy's heart sank again. 'Where is she?'

'Don't rightly know. Gone out with Dennis, I think. And Michelle's over at her friends. You know Joanne?'

'Er ... no.' What should I do now, Ziggy wondered. What if they're going to be out late. 'Will she be back later do you think?'

'Oh yes. She's usually in by ten.'

Ziggy looked across at the digital clock. 19.31. By the time he got up there, if he got up there, it would be nearly ten anyway. His Auntie Ann brought his attention back to the phone. 'That's a bit late for you, isn't it?'

'Er . . . yeah.'

'I'll tell her you called though.'

'OK.'

'You going to try again tomorrow?'

'Er . . . yeah. I might try later. Er . . . in case she comes in early like.'

'Oh. . . . Rightee oh then.'

So far so good, Ziggy thought. Everything's still going according to plan. However, as he formulated the thought in his head everything almost fell to pieces. Just as his Auntie Ann started to speak, so did the Airport Public Address system. 'British Airways announce the final call for flight BA5620, the 1955 to Aberdeen. This flight is now closing. Any remaining passengers should go immediately to Gate Number 12.'

As the announcement was repeated Ziggy could hardly hear himself speak, never mind his Auntie Ann.

'Eric . . . Eric. What was that?'

Oh God, thought Ziggy. What else could it be? The bubble's about to burst.

'It's . . . it's, er . . . the telly, Auntie Ann.' As he said it Ziggy realised it was the wrong thing to say.

'Where are you?' she demanded. She knew they didn't have their own phone.

'Er – I'm at me mate's home. Someone I know from school.'

'It's a very loud television, isn't it. All of a sudden, like.'

'I . . . er . . . I sat on the remote control thing. Put the volume up, you know.'

'Hhmmm. Are you sure you're not up to something you shouldn't be?'

'No. Of course not.'

'I'll of course not you, me lad. I know you of old.'

'What would I be doing?' God, Ziggy moaned to himself, I'll have to try and bluff this out. Why did I bother making this call anyway. Another bloody announcement will go off in a minute. Then what.

'You're not out in a pub or anything, are you?'

'No. Of course . . . I mean . . . no . . . honest.' Good old Auntie Ann. She's going for the obvious. It might even be worth saying I am. She'd accept that and just moan the next time she spoke to me ma. I'll have to get off this phone anyway.

'Er . . . I'm all right, Auntie. Honest. I'll have to go. Me money's running out.'

'Thought you said you was in your friend's house.'

'Er . . . I am.' Ziggy's heart went heavy again. The pips! She'll hear the bloody pips, won't she. 'I'll have to go, though. Me mate's dad'll do his nut if I run up a big bill, won't he.' Ziggy hoped she would understand that. She did.

'Oh . . . yes. Of course.'

'OK then. I'll see ya.' He tried to put the phone down but his auntie kept talking.

'Before you go, Eric. How's your mum and dad?'

'Fine.' Ziggy glanced at the digital clock. 19.33. The pips would go any second.

'See ya, Auntie.'

'What about school?'

'Oh, it's great. Look – I'll have to go.' He noticed the 'INSERT MONEY' indicator flashing on the phone. Oh, God. She'll hear the pips.

He wanted to hang up but he knew he couldn't. If he did she would get suspicious. He had to finish naturally. Well, as naturally as he could. 'Everything's great, Auntie. I just wanted to talk to Allie about something. I'll try and phone later, but if not I'll call her tomorrow. OK?'

'Yeah. OK. Give my love to your mum and dad.'

'Yeah,' he said. I will if you get off the phone before the pips, he thought. 'Yeah. I will. See you.'

'Bye, Eric. God bless.' With that there was a click. She had put the phone down. Almost at the same time Ziggy heard the rapid pips telling him to do as the flashing indicator requested – INSERT MORE MONEY. No chance, he thought as he dropped the receiver back on to its cradle. He let out a long sigh and became aware of the sweat on his hands, back and forehead. That had been a close one.

The bubble was still intact. The incredible journey was still on, but where was BD590? That was the next thing to figure out!

ELEVEN

While Ziggy was still trying to find BD590, Gonch was standing on top of an old packing case, trying to figure out which hole in the wall they should follow.

Hollo was still sitting on one of the hundreds of pipes that ran round the room. He was still rubbing his elbow. 'You might have caught me,' he moaned to Gonch.

'No one caught me,' Gonch replied. 'And I didn't hurt myself, either.'

Hollo could see he wasn't going to get any sympathy from Gonch. He was too interested in all the pipes.

'It must be one of these big ones here,' said Gonch.

'Why?'

Gonch sighed but then said, 'Look. If these boilers have to heat the whole school, then they're going to need big pipes to carry all the hot water and stuff round the school, aren't they?'

'Yeah. Or bring it back.'

'What?'

Now Hollo sighed. 'If the water goes out hot, it'll cool down eventually won't it. So it's got to come back here to be heated up again. You know. Back to the central heating boiler. That's why they call it. . . .'

'All right . . . all right. You've made your point,' Gonch grumbled.

'So which one's hot?' Hollo asked.

'This one,' said Gonch, pointing to a pipe.

'So that must be the start of the system,' stated Hollo quite confidently.

'So is this one!' Gonch announced. Hollo looked less confident. 'And this one. And this.' Hollo looked even less confident as all the pipes Gonch pointed to went off in different directions.

'Now what?' Gonch finally asked.

Hollo just shrugged. He was at a loss for what to do next. Instead he concentrated on the obstacles in their path. 'Anyway,' he said, 'how are we going to get through those? They're too narrow.' He pointed to the small openings through which the pipes disappeared. There was only about half a metre of space between the pipes and the side of the holes.

'They might widen out,' suggested Gonch, more from hope than anything else. If only I could see a bit past these pipes. See where these ducts go.'

'They could go anywhere, couldn't they? How'd we know we'll come up near the Staff Room?'

'We don't have to come up near the Staff Room. All we need do is get into the school, clown.'

Hollo nodded. Gonch was right. Again. 'Didn't you bring a torch?' he asked.

'Oh yeah. I always carry a torch in case I decide to go pot-holing or something.

'I only asked.'

'Yeah. A stupid question.' Gonch then looked around the boiler room. 'Old Griffiths must have a torch somewhere.'

'Probably taken it home to polish,' Hollo suggested as he got up to have a look. No sign, although he did find a few old candles and a box of matches near a fuse box. 'What about these? He must keep 'em for emergencies.'

74

'Yeah. They'll do. Toss us one up.'

Hollo threw a candle and a box of matches up to Gonch, who soon lit the candle and was back peering into the gloom of the central heating duct. 'Great!' Gonch suddenly exclaimed.

'What?' Hollo enquired.

'It's only narrow at the top here. This wall's only 200 millimetres thick. Then it widens out into about a metre square duct.'

'How far can you see?'

'About three metres. Then it turns a corner.'

Hollo looked about the room to take his bearings from the coal chute they had slid down. 'That must be . . . that must be under the Woodwork room then.'

'Yeah,' Gonch agreed. 'So if it turns right there and goes straight on it should cross the corridor outside the Woodwork room, shouldn't it?'

Hollo agreed, although without that much enthusiasm. The more he thought about crawling along the ducts the more he didn't fancy the idea. 'You think there's rats in there?' he asked Gonch.

Gonch stopped his peering routine. He hadn't thought of that. 'Er . . . no. Of course not.' He didn't sound too convinced.

'Or what about a gas leak?' Hollo enquired. 'We shouldn't go in there with a naked flame. We might blow ourselves to bits.'

'There's no gas in there.'

'How'd you know? We use gas in the labs, don't we. It's got to get there somehow, hasn't it?'

Gonch paused. Hollo had a point. 'Where's the gas meter?' he suddenly asked.

Hollo looked around. 'Can't see one,' he said. 'But

these boilers are gas, aren't they? All central heating is gas, isn't it?'

'No. Ours isn't. Ours is electric.'

'That's expensive, though. So me dad says. The school wouldn't have electric.'

'No, suppose not.' Gonch was beginning to worry that they had hit a real problem when he remembered seeing the tanker the day before.

'It's oil, clown. They deliver oil don't they?'

'Oh yeah,' conceded Hollo. 'But there's still gas in the labs.'

'But no gas meter in here. Right?' Gonch asked.

'Right.' Hollo agreed.

'Then there can't be any gas pipes running from here into those ducts.'

'No. . . .' Hollo could see Gonch's point, but he wasn't going to be convinced so easily. 'It has to get in somewhere. It could come in round that bend you can see.'

'Yeah, but it's more likely to come in straight by the labs, isn't it? On the far side of the school.' Gonch was now adamant. There was no real danger from a gas leak. 'Are you coming or not?'

Hollo knew he didn't really have a choice. He'd come this far. 'What about rats, though?' he asked as he found himself once again following Gonch through the hole in the wall.

'I'll let you know if I see any.'

'How?'

'You'll see me die of fright. OK?'

This brought a smile to Hollo's face as he scrambled into the duct, and fell a short way on to the floor as it widened out. He hurt his elbow again. 'Why didn't you warn me about that?' he moaned at Gonch.

76

'You never asked,' hissed Gonch as he turned the bend and disappeared. With him went the candle, leaving Hollo in pitch darkness except for the dim light of the entrance to the duct in the boiler room. No matter how nervous he felt about rats and gas explosions, Hollo didn't want to be left behind in the dark. He scrambled on and round the bend after Gonch.

'See anything?' Hollo called.

'Spiders!' Gonch replied.

'Spiders I can cope with. It's . . . uurrgghh.' Hollo stopped. He had just put his knee in something wet and soggy. 'What's that?'

'Oh – watch out. There's a puddle of water or something there,' Gonch annnounced. A little too late.

'Thanks a lot. Give us the candle then, so I can see what the damage is.'

'Hang on.'

'What?' Hollo picked up the excitement in Gonch's voice.

'Here's a manhole cover.'

Hollo immediately forgot his wet trousers.

'Can you open it?'

Gonch pushed and pushed. Then let out a long sigh. 'No. It seems to be locked. Better carry on to the next one.'

Hollo automatically followed. 'Where do you reckon we are now?'

'Dunno. Somewhere by the canteen I think. We must have passed Woodwork and the Home Economics rooms by now.'

'What's that!?' Hollo suddenly shouted.

'What!?' Gonch was so startled he banged his head

on the roof of the duct. 'What is it?' he asked Hollo, who was now crouching against the opposite side of the duct.

'There. Down there,' Hollo pointed. 'Something furry. It moved. It's a rat. I know it is.'

Gonch moved the candle round. He hoped it wasn't a rat. It was there. Just behind the bracket that held one of the pipes to the wall. Did it move? He edged closer, holding the candle out in front. Then he laughed and reached out and picked up the mysterious object.

'What is it?' Hollo asked nervously.

'Here. Catch!' Gonch thew it to Hollo. Hollo screamed. It would be just like Gonch to toss him a dead rat. He felt the object land on his shoulder and was almost too petrified to look, until he realised Gonch was falling about laughing. It was an old piece of rag. 'Very funny!' Hollo spat as he threw the rag back.

He could have sworn it had been a rat. How stupid can you get, he thought. I'm letting my mind run away with me. It might have been only a piece of rag, but as he moved on after Gonch he thought he heard a noise. Was there something else out there in the dark? 'Gonch!' he called. 'Wait for me!'

They tried three more manholes before they eventually found one that opened. It came up in the girls' changing room in the Gym. But the changing room door was locked, as it always was. They had no choice but to go back down the duct and keep looking. However, as their search continued they found they had another problem. They were hopelessly lost.

They had come across several points where the duct met others. At these junctions they sometimes had a choice of about four different directions in which to go. Hollo was becoming more and more convinced that they were going round in circles. He looked at his watch. It was just after half past seven. They had been scrabbling around in the dark for over an hour. What was worse, the candle was nearly burnt out. It was bad enough trying to see as it was. Without the candle it would be hopeless.

'What happens if we can't find our way back to the boiler room?' Hollo asked. There was a touch of desperation in his voice.

'We will,' Gonch replied. He didn't sound too confident.

'We're going round in circles, aren't we? There's nothing to show us where we are. Or where we've been.'

'I suppose you're going to ask me if I brought some chalk, or a ball of string so we could leave a trail behind us.'

'No,' said Hollo. Then added. 'But it would help.'

'And so would you stopping moaning.'

'I'm not moaning. I'm just saying we're lost.'

'I know that, don't I?' Then he stopped. He had found another manhole cover. 'Let's try this one.'

'What's the point? They're all locked. Probably to stop us getting into here during the day.'

Gonch ignored him and shoved at the cover. Did it move? He thought it did.

'It moved!' he shouted.

'Did it?' Hollo was immediately by his side.

'Push!'

The two mates put all their effort and weight behind the push and the cover lifted. They came up into a corridor and to their great surprise and

79

excitement they found they were immediately outside the Staff Room, a few metres away from Gonch's Walkman. They tried the door and their surprise and excitement continued to rise as they discovered it was open. And then the surprise reached a new height – not of excitement but of horror – as bells started to ring all over the school. They had set off the burglar alarms!!

TWELVE

The digital clock changed to 19.45. The VDU's changed to say BD590 should board at Gate 50. Yet Ziggy still couldn't figure out which airline it was.

He had walked up and down the building looking for clues but had had no success. For a few moments he thought he had solved the mystery following another flight announcement over the public address system. He had heard British Airways make a final announcement for 'the two remaining passengers for flight BA5620 to go immediately to Gate 12 as the flight was now closing.' He had worked out that everyone had to go through one gate to get to the planes. But to get there you had to pass a security guard. And you had to have a ticket. He had also worked out that a boarding card for the British Airways shuttle service to Manchester, Edinburgh or Glasgow would do. He also noticed that you could get these boarding cards at the Super-shuttle counter.

Ziggy knew a bit about the shuttle service as they had done a project on airlines in the last year of his primary school. He knew they were supposed to be more like a train or bus than a plane – you could roll up on the day and pay as you got on, or something like that, he remembered.

So, the shuttle boarding card would get me past the bloke on the door, he thought as he went over the problem again. Except I don't want to go to Manchester, Edinburgh or Glasgow. I want to go to Liverpool and British Airways don't go there. Which airline did?

He had almost given up when the answer was presented to him. By the same public address system that had nearly burst the bubble when he was speaking on the phone to his Auntie Ann.

'British Midland announce the departure of flight BD340 to Teeside. All passengers for this flight should go now to Gate Number 4. British Midland announce. . . .'

Ziggy didn't wait to listen to the rest of the announcement. That was it. BD was British Midland. He didn't understand why it wasn't BM, but he didn't care. He now knew which airline flew to Liverpool. He now knew where he had to go. All he had to do was do it.

Easier said than done, he thought, as he walked as calmly and as normally as possible to the shuttle desk and picked up a boarding card. He checked his timetable. There was a Manchester flight at 20.30. That would do to get him past the guard. But then his own thoughts came back to him. I'm an obvious target being alone. He'll suss me out in the same way the bloke at Euston Station did.

He looked round. There was no woman struggling with suitcases and kids. The place seemed filled with business men in suits. None of them needed help with their briefcases. Kids! That's it, thought Ziggy. He spun on his heel. Where was that shop I saw. His thoughts raced as quickly as he did through the building. I'll go and get some stuff and pretend . . . yeah . . . that should do it. Get back. Pick me moment. Yeah. Gotcha!!!

He was still grinning as he returned, puffing a bit

from the running, towards the security entrance. The puffin' will help, and all, Ziggy thought as he slotted into the middle of a group of business suits. Looks like I've been told to hurry up and that. Suddenly he was in front of the security guard, who hardly seemed to look at everyone else's ticket, but put his hand out for Ziggy's.

Ziggy felt his throat go dry as he offered the guy the shuttle boarding card. As Ziggy suspected, it wasn't enough.

'Where's your ticket, son?'

'Er . . . me ma's got it.'

'And where's she?' The security guard asked looking back over Ziggy's shoulder into the growing queue of people.

'Er . . . she's in there. In the er . . . place you get the shuttles. I'm . . . er . . . we're going to Manchester.' It didn't sound convincing.

'Are you now? So why aren't you with your mother?'

'She sent me back out to get this stuff.' He played his ace card as he held up a packet of tissues and a packet of cotton wool balls. He could see the guards eyes flicker. He was beginning to accept it. 'They're for the baby. She had an accident.' The guard was going for it, so Ziggy pushed. He gambled that the guard wouldn't remember half the people who passed him. The size of the queue building up behind convinced him of that. 'We went through before.'

'Then why haven't you got a ticket?'

'Er . . . it happened before we bought them – she just told me to go. And hurry up. The baby'll be screamin' by now!' And it won't be the only one, Ziggy thought, as he listened to the level of muttering and moaning growing from behind him.

'What's going on?' somebody shouted.

'Come along. I've got a plane to catch, you know,' another man added.

What else would he be wanting to catch Ziggy thought quickly, without taking his eyes off the security guard. It was important not to look away. Look confident. Look ordinary. Look normal.

Whether it was his own Oscar-winning performance or whether it was the growing complaints from the queue behind him, Ziggy never knew. Whatever it was it was enough. The security guard nodded and Ziggy found he was past the first obstacle.

He didn't look back as he hurried away and along a kind of glassed-in bridge that went over a road. His eyes were searching for clues to Gate 50. He saw a VDU immediately in front telling him that BD590 was still boarding at Gate 50. Then he saw the sign for Gate 50 itself – down a long ramp to his left.

Instinctively he glanced back to where the security guard was sitting. He wasn't looking. Even if he was he probably couldn't have seen Ziggy as all the people that formed the queue during Ziggy's interrogation flowed through.

Ziggy dashed off down the ramp. It was quite steep and after about 15 metres it turned left and doubled back on itself. It was like going down a giant helter-skelter. He was now at ground level and headed off to find Gate 50. He followed the glass wall until he was level with where the ramp had turned back on itself, now above him. He could only go in one direction – however he stopped dead in his tracks. Then he quickly ducked back behind the ramp supports.

In front of him was a greater obstacle than the

84

security guard upstairs. He took another quick peek round the corner. There was a short queue of about four people, waiting to present their tickets and select their seats. In front of them were two uniformed officials of the airline. Everyone had to go past these two, through a small opening between two counters. If that wasn't impossible in itself, behind that was another counter where three security guards were checking everyone's luggage and making them pass through some kind of detector thing. Beyond that he could see all the passengers sitting in a small lounge.

That was enough for Ziggy. He knew he'd never even get past the first counter. There was no way. And even if he did and then got past the second counter they could see everyone in the lounge. They'd see he wasn't with anyone. It was no use. Absolutely no use.

He turned and hurried off the way he came. He hurried up the helter-skelter ramp, passing a few more business suits going in the opposite direction. As he approached the top he began to worry about the security guard again.

What if he sees me coming up here? Ziggy thought. He'll know I'm up to something, won't he? If he's looking he's bound to see me. He was now nearly at the top of the ramp. Just act natural. Be ordinary. Be normal. He kept telling himself this as he slowed down at the top of the ramp. But what now? Which way shall I go? What shall I do?

The answer to these questions came when he saw in the distance a sign for the British Airways shuttle. Manchester, he thought. He glanced at the VDU at the top of the ramp. BA4532 2030 BOARD GATE 5. Even before he considered it he found himself heading down the corridor toward Gate 5. The shuttle lounge.

If it's just the same I'll jack it in, he told himself as he approached the entrance door. I've still got more than enough to get home on the train. Hey, what about getting from Manchester to Liverpool. How'll I do that? For a moment he was filled with dread again. What's the point of going through all this and being stranded in Manchester? Nah, don't be soft. There's bound to be a train from Manchester to Liverpool. If you can get a train from London you're bound to be able to get one from Manchester. He checked the money in his pocket again. Yeah. That should be enough. It'll be nowhere near as dear as travelling from London, will it. And I'll be able to cadge the return fare from our Allie. Yeah. Come 'ead, Zig, lad. You haven't done all this to give up now.

He might not have wanted to give up there and then, but his heart nearly did as he reached the entrance to the shuttle lounge.

Ziggy froze. He didn't know what to do. He was terrified to go on as he was bound to be questioned and caught out by all these guards.

But not for long. He thawed out quite suddenly when one of the guards stepped forward.

'No luggage, son?'

'Er . . . no . . .' Ziggy stammered. He had to go on with his story. He held up the cotton wool. 'Me ma's got it. In there. She er . . . sent me for these. For the baby.' God, I shouldn't have said that, Ziggy thought. They might not have had a baby in here. He could feel his throat drying up again as well as the sweat forming on his back. It was suddenly beginning to itch again as well.

'Over here, then,' the security guard suddenly spoke.

Where? Ziggy's thoughts raced ahead of his eyes as he began to imagine being taken to one side. Taken into a small room. Questioned. Arrested. However, before his mind had him in court, sentenced and sent to prison, his eyes had followed the security guard to the same kind of detector he had seen at Gate 50.

Almost without realising Ziggy found himself being guided through it. He waited for the security guard to arrest him. But he didn't. He just smiled and turned away to deal with the next passenger. Ziggy couldn't believe it. He was through another barrier. The next one was trying to get on to the plane without a ticket. How could he do that?

He needed time to think and time to watch what was going on so he decided to have a problem with his trainers. While he was fixing the laces and searching for the stone inside, he watched people go up and buy their tickets. They got them from one counter and then took them to another where they could choose a seat. They then went through into the lounge properly where they could buy a drink, coffee or newspaper while they waited for the plane.

Ziggy moved a bit closer to the counters where they gave out the seats. There was a sign above each counter. One for Edinburgh. One for Glasgow and one for Manchester. Ziggy also noticed that when people handed in their tickets they got back a boarding card like the one he had, except that it had a little sticker with the seat number on it. That's what I need, he thought to himself. But it was obvious there would be no way he could get his hands on one. There were too many people knocking about.

Anyway, he thought, I can't fiddle with me trainers all night. He looked back at the security guards. They were all busy searching luggage. He looked at the staff on the counters. They all seemed occupied, so he decided to take the bull by the horns and have a go. He just stood up and walked toward the Manchester counter. He waved his boarding card, making sure to keep the side that should have the sticker on it facing toward him. To his amazement no one stopped him. Everyone assumed that as he had got this far he must be a genuine passenger.

Ziggy couldn't believe his luck. He was actually in the shuttle lounge itself. He had got through four barriers. He realised he still had a few more to go, but he had got this far at least. He looked around the metal and chrome lounge. There were a lot of staff – both airline and security. Ziggy realised that although the lounge was busy, he would soon stand out by himself. He noticed a digital clock displaying 20.02. Nearly half-an-hour to wait – to be natural – to be ordinary – to be normal. He looked around – where else could be more normal than the loo? He dashed off toward the gents.

THIRTEEN

Back at Grange Hill Gonch and Hollo were terrified. Ziggy was petrified in the Heathrow Airport toilets, while Julia was scared stiff in St Saviour's toilets. She and Laura were helping the police with their enquiries. And those enquiries were taking ages. It was now five past eight. They would be late getting back to the Library.

'Why can't you say anything?' the policewoman asked once again. Laura could see she was beginning to lose patience with Julia.

'Look,' Laura said. 'Does it really matter? We've got all the money back.' She knew it did matter. She knew the police would want to try and catch Imelda and her cronies. She knew what trouble this whole thing would cause for Julia if her father found out. She also knew it was all her fault. She had wanted to come to the Jumble Sale. She had persuaded Julia to come. She had also told her to tell lies. She had a lot to answer for.

'That's not the point,' the policewoman said, starting to examine the window. 'These people need to be caught. If they came in through this window, as seems likely, they probably left some fingerprints. If you give us a clear description, we might know who they are, mightn't we? So, why can't you tell me?'

Julia remained silent. How could she say that she couldn't help catch the obnoxious Imelda because she was frightened of her own father? It sounded so ridiculous.

89

The policewoman, of course, knew none of this and she was beginning to lose patience. 'Anymore of this,' she said, 'and I'll begin to think you two were in on this robbery.'

Julia turned pale – and Laura turned red. This was getting out of hand.

'How?' Laura exclaimed. 'How can you possibly think that? She tried to warn everyone. She threw a trifle at them. And me!'

'It could have been to create a diversion,' the policewoman said calmly, still examining the broken window catch.

'Some diversion,' Laura sneered. She felt that same irritation and anger she had felt earlier with the woman whose foot she'd trodden on. How can adults act so childishly. 'Shouting about the robbery itself? Throwing a trifle at our so-called accomplices? If we'd have been involved, wouldn't we have tried to get people to look the other way?

'You're being insolent,' the policewoman said.

'You're being silly,' Laura replied.

'Why won't you co-operate?'

'Because we're not supposed to be here!' Laura suddenly blurted out. She could have bitten her tongue. Instead she threw her head back and spun round on her heel. Damn. Damn. Damn. She then turned to apologise to Julia, but couldn't say anything when she saw the look on her face. It was the policewoman who spoke next.

'Oh . . .' she said. 'And why not?'

Laura exchanged a look with Julia, who must have seen the look of regret on her face because she nodded and gave a faint smile.

'My dad doesn't like me going out at night,' Julia

said to the policewoman.

'Very sensible of him. But where are you supposed to be tonight then? If not here?'

'The Library.'

The policewoman nodded. She soon realised exactly what the problem was. 'And if you talk to us, he'll find out? Is that it?'

Julia exchanged another look with Laura and then nodded. Oh why, she thought. Why did I let Laura talk me into this in the first place?

'And what if you continue to refuse to talk to us. What then?' the policewoman asked. 'Have you thought of that?'

Julia didn't understand. She looked to Laura.

'How? How do you mean?' Laura asked.

'Well. What if I decided you two were acting so suspiciously that I had to take you down to the station to help with our enquiries.' The two girls looked horrified. The policewoman continued. 'You'd have to tell us then or be kept there all night. Your father would be bound to find out about that now, wouldn't he?'

Julia couldn't believe it. A few hours ago they had been eating toast in her bedroom and having a good laugh. Now she was faced with the prospect of being locked up in a police cell all night.

'You ... er ... you wouldn't do that, would you?' she asked the policewoman.

'It might teach you a good lesson,' the police-woman replied.

'It's already done that,' responded Julia, throwing a less than friendly glance at Laura.

The policewoman picked it up. 'Your idea, was it? All this?' she asked Laura.

'Yes, I'm afraid so,' replied Laura. 'It was all harmless, really. We planned to be back at the Library by 8.30 so Julia's father could pick us up.'

'Oh . . . your name's Julia, is it?'

Laura did bite her tongue this time. She'd done it again. What an idiot.

'Yes,' answered Julia. 'And hers is Laura. Laura Reagan.'

'Thanks a lot,' said Laura. She didn't really mind. She didn't blame Julia. She'd caused her a lot of trouble.

'And what's *your* second name?' the policewoman asked Julia.

Julia hesitated for an instant. Threw another look at Laura, then said. 'Glover. Julia Glover.'

The policewoman wrote both down. 'And what school do you go to?' she asked without really expecting a reply. She was surprised to hear Laura speak.

'Grange Hill. My mother's a teacher there.'

'And my father is one of the school governors,' Julia added. The girls had both decided that neither of them wanted to spend a night in the cells.

'I see,' said the policewoman. 'And do any of the people you saw trying to steal the money go to Grange Hill?'

The girls hesitated. Julia looked to Laura – she wanted her to take the lead again. Laura hesitated. She didn't know what to do. If she said who it was there would be no question that Julia's father would definitely hear about it all as a school governor. At the moment there was still a slim chance he wouldn't need to know. If they co-operated with the police they might not need to tell their parents anything. So long as they kept it away from the school.

'Well?' the policewoman urged.

Laura was still undecided as to what to do for the best, when there was a knock on the toilet door. A voice called out. 'Is it safe to enter?' It was a man's voice.

'Yes. Come in,' said the policewoman.

The door opened and in walked the vicar of St Saviour's Church. Although his face carried a huge grin, he was quite uncomfortable entering the Ladies' toilet, and his walk was more of an embarrassed shuffle. 'Er ... er ... how are things going with ... er ... our two saviours?' he asked, smiling at his own joke. Laura, Julia and the policewoman managed a smile, more out of politeness than appreciation of the humour.

The policewoman was about to speak, but the vicar was obviously excited and wanted to continue. 'Well,' he said. 'everything's fine outside. The trifle's a ... er ... trifle messy,' he grinned again. 'But,' the vicar continued, 'it's all cleaned up. Everyone's calmed down. And as far as we can tell God's been kind to us. We're only 20p short on the raffle money. Amazing, don't you think? All that money scattered everywhere. And only 20p goes missing. Remarkable. Remarkable, isn't it?' It was a general question for them all – not aimed at anyone in particular, so none of them made a reply. Which probably suited the vicar as he immediately continued, 'And what's happening in here? Any progress?'

'Oh, not too good I'm afraid,' said the policewoman.

'Oh,' said the vicar, rather surprised.

'Failing memories,' the policewoman said. 'We come across it all the time.'

'Oh,' said the vicar. 'That happens to me all the time.' He looked at the two girls. He could sense rather than see that there was something wrong. 'Especially when it might cause me some trouble.' He could see by the exchange of looks between Laura and Julia that he had hit the target. 'What's the problem?' he asked. 'Parents not know where you are?'

Laura smiled and shook her head. 'I see,' the vicar said and turned to the policewoman. 'Ah well, no real harm done in there. We've got all our money back – except 20p.'

'That's not the point,' the policewoman said.

'No ... true. True,' said the vicar. 'But what use is there in getting these two young ladies into trouble? It would be a shame if their good deed turned sour on them. After all,' he winked at the girls, 'they might never help anyone again if that were to happen.'

You're certainly right there, thought Julia. She then looked pleadingly at the policewoman, who was hesitating, so the vicar started to talk again. 'After all,' he said, 'they've probably learnt quite a lesson tonight.' The two girls nodded. 'And we here ourselves, were very silly. This window should have been locked. And better care should have been taken over the money. Very lax. Very lax. Especially in this day and age. I'm just delighted that we had these two honest and caring people with us tonight. That's what we should be really thankful for.' All right, vicar, Laura thought. I know you're trying to talk her round, but don't lay it on too thick. She looked at the policewoman. She was actually putting her notebook away. It had worked.

'OK. OK,' the policewoman said. 'I know when

94

I'm beaten.' She turned to the girls. 'Go on. You'd better get off to the Library as fast as you can!'

The two girls exchanged a look. It took a moment to sink in. When it did they both turned and moved to the door. 'Well,' said the policewoman. 'Aren't you going to thank the vicar?'

The girls stopped. 'Thanks,' said Laura.

'Yes, thank you,' said Julia.

'No. I should be thanking you,' the vicar said.

'Oh . . .' said Julia, with a grin, 'it was nothing. A mere trifle.'

The vicar and the policewoman groaned and Julia dashed out. Laura stopped and put her hand in her pocket, pulled out 20p and gave it to the vicar. 'I hope you get the mini-bus,' she said, and dashed out after Julia.

The vicar and the policewoman exchanged a look, then smiled. He looked at the 20p and said, 'I think you made the right decision there.'

'Yes,' said the policewoman. 'I wouldn't have done it if they hadn't been decent kids. And,' she grinned again, 'I think when they get to the Library they'll learn a bigger lesson than they would from us.'

The vicar looked puzzled. He wouldn't have done if he had seen the looks of horror on the girls' faces as they dashed round the corner and came to a sliding stop outside the Library. It was closed! It had been for a week. They were repainting it.

'Oh, no!' exclaimed Julia.

'Oh, yes,' said a voice. The girls spun round to find Julia's father standing behind them.

'You've got a bit of explaining to do, my girl. There's the car. Get in.'

He pointed to the car. The two girls climbed into

the back. Julia turned to Laura as she watched her father walk round the front of the car to get in the driver's door. 'Do me a favour, Laura,' she said.

'What?'

'Let me do the explaining this time. OK?'

'OK.'

The two girls sank down into the seat. They felt that this was going to be the most unpleasant ride home they had ever had.

FOURTEEN

The alarm bells were still ringing at Grange Hill. Laura and Julia were riding home in silence with Mr Glover, while Ziggy was still trying to work out a way to get on to the plane without a ticket.

At first, after he locked himself in the toilet cubicle, Ziggy had planned to go out into the lounge and see if he could 'acquire' a boarding card with a seat sticker. He had decided that some people were bound to leave them on the seats when they went for a coffee, a newspaper or even to the toilet. If they did he might be able to swop his blank card. He might be able to get on the plane that way. He might – if he could find enough strength and courage to get out of the cubicle. At the moment he couldn't. He was too scared.

The last time Ziggy had spent so much time in the toilet was at primary school when Solly Benson had been looking for him. He had never been so scared since then, either. Although he didn't have to keep his legs pulled up on the pan this time, he had that same feeling in his stomach. That sort of empty sinking feeling as every opening and closing of the door, every footstep outside might be the one. The one that meant discovery.

Ziggy could never remember why Solly had decided to go for him. Solly probably didn't even know himself. Solly was like that. Ziggy was convinced that Solly didn't have one brain cell anywhere in his body, never mind his head. This view had been supported by most of the school. Particularly when Solly was often seen trying to see if he could smash a hole in the boiler house door with his head. When Solly came after him Ziggy had had to stay locked in the toilet for about two hours. He didn't get out until his form teacher came to find him and escorted him home.

What a headcase, Ziggy thought, shaking his head at the memory of Solly. Mind you, I can talk, can't I? What am I doing sitting here? I must be a grade one bone brain, I must. I've got this far, but what am I supposed to do now? They're bound to twig on the plane, aren't they? Especially if they count heads.

Ziggy had gone quite sick when he started to wonder if they counted how many people were on board the plane. He had decided they must do as he remembered an announcement he had heard earlier for 'the last two remaining passengers'. He had asked himself how they knew there were two remaining. It was obvious: they counted people on board. They then compared that with the number of tickets sold. Any less on board meant people were missing. Any more and . . . God, moaned Ziggy. How'd I get meself into this? And what if all the tickets have been sold? What if the plane is full? They won't have to count heads then, will they. They'll bloody well find me standing in the aisle, won't they.

Despite these fears Ziggy had worked out a plan. He had heard an announcement that they would put people on to the plane by rows, starting at the back of the plane. Ziggy thought that if he waited until near the end to sneak on, most people would have their seats and only the empty ones would be left. After that he could keep a look out to see if anyone was counting. If they were he would try to hide or move about and hope they missed him. He had then revised his plan when he realised that if he waited until the very end he would be too conspicuous. If would be best to try and slip on board somewhere in the middle.

Suddenly he heard another announcement. 'Ladies and Gentlemen. Your Super Shuttle service to Manchester is now ready for boarding. Will those passengers in seats 10 to 25 please board at Gate A.'

That's it, thought Ziggy. It's now or never. That's the middle of the plane. He found himself asking himself, shall I go or not? Once again he found his body answering the question before his mind was ready – he was going for the biggey.

All I need is a bit of luck, he thought, as he stepped back to let another businessman enter. Ziggy watched the man cross over towards the urinals and put his briefcase down near the sinks. On top of it was a boarding card, and on the boarding card was a sticker with a seat number.

Ziggy suddenly felt the need to check his trainers again. He also managed to check that the boarding card was for Manchester. The seat number was 18C, one of the rows just called on the announcement. That was exactly what Ziggy needed. It was also exactly what Ziggy got.

As the man finished at the urinal, he turned toward the sink to wash his hands. He didn't notice Ziggy exit. He finished, picked up his briefcase, Ziggy's boarding card and left the toilet.

It was only outside in the lounge that the man realised something was wrong. Ziggy could see him stop as he glanced at the boarding card and realised it was blank. The man looked on the floor as though he might have droppped the other card. He then turned and went back into the toilets.

By the time the man reappeared looking totally mystified, Ziggy was on board the plane. He had joined the queue of passengers and handed in the man's boarding card. It was all like he'd seen on the telly. He didn't have any trouble. He just followed the crowd and walked down the plane toward the back.

The plane had three seats on either side of the centre aisle, so Ziggy worked out that 18C must be third from the end of the row. A.B.C. 1.2.3. He found seat 18C but decided not to use it. There might be a record with the man's ticket. He decided to stick to his original plan and head for the back of the plane. Sure enough he found two empty rows of seats on one side with lots of others dotted about. He slid into one of them and squashed himself up against the window, as low as he possibly could. All he had to do now was watch out for the head counting.

A stewardess passed down the aisle from the back to the front so she didn't notice Ziggy, now almost crouching on the floor. However her passing made Ziggy sit up. Idiot, he thought to himself. Act natural. Ordinary. Normal. Anyone on their own is going to be suspicious, but someone crouching under a seat is going to be a dead give away, isn't he. Ziggy forced himself to sit up straight. He then fished in his pocket and took out what was left of the man's boarding card. When he had got on they had torn it in two and given him a bit back. 18C. He looked up to find his own seat number. It was 27A. Behind him Row 28 was empty. He had an idea. He took the seat sticker off the boarding card and tore it in half so that only the 8C remained. Next he stuck it back on the card. No, it didn't look right. He then decided to tear the boarding card beneath the sticker, to make it look as though the 2 of 28 had been torn off when they tore his card in half. Flicking the other pieces as far away as possible, he stood up and quickly changed seats. And crossed his fingers.

Everyone seemed to be settling down and Ziggy was beginning to feel a little bit more optimistic. The last of the passengers seemed to have boarded the plane. Even the man whose boarding card Ziggy had taken was back on board – sitting in seat 18C. Obviously he had got on because of his ticket, and it was also obvious to Ziggy that they did keep a record of who sat in each seat.

He was so absorbed in watching the man in case he turned round and recognised him that he didn't notice the woman standing in the aisle next to him.

She had walked up the plane looking for her seat, and it was her voice that made Ziggy's heart nearly jump out of his chest. 'Excuse me. But aren't you sitting in my seat, young man?'

Ziggy froze. No muscle in his body would work. All he could hear was a voice in his head saying, 'This is it. This is it.' The woman obviously thought he was some form of mental retard as she poked him on the shoulder. 'Do you hear me? You're sitting in my seat.' All Ziggy could do was stare at her and make strange noises in his throat as his brain tried to regain control of his muscles. He was caught. That was it.

The woman, however, was beginning to lose patience with the sub-normal being in front of her. 'Look. If you can't understand what I'm saying. Perhaps you can read. Look. 27C. See 27C.'

Ziggy did look. As he did, he felt a warm wave of relief wash over him. *She* was in the wrong seat. Not him. 'Er . . . er . . . you . . . er . . .' his brain was beginning to win the fight to regain control. 'Er . . . you're in the wrong seat, missus,' he heard himself say. Keep it up. Keep it up, he urged. He heard himself speak. Saw himself hold up his torn boarding card. Saw himself point to the 8C. 'This is 28C. That's 27C.'

'Oh!' the woman said. 'Oh . . . sorry. So sorry.' She then moved and sat down. Ziggy could have kissed her. However his passion for this unknown woman didn't last long as Ziggy spotted a stewardess walking slowly up the aisle. Counting heads! His 8C trick wouldn't work again. He took a quick look round, but there was nowhere to go. If he tried to move she would see him anyway. Then the count would be one too many. They would probably stop the plane until they found out who it was. Act natural. Ordinary. Normal. No way, he thought. He slid off his seat and rolled himself into a ball under the row in front.

He never knew how he managed it. Sheer panic, he concluded later. However, the stewardess passed. The head count was right. He heard all the doors close. He felt the plane moving. He heard the cabin crew demonstrating what to do with the life jackets in an emergency. Some good that's going to do me, he thought before his heart skipped another beat as he heard them mention that the life jackets were kept under the seats. I hope no one wants to look under this one, he thought. The next thing he felt was the plane taxiing out to the runway. He heard the engines roar and felt the plane pick up speed and felt himself sliding backwards along the floor as it lifted off.

Panic. Fortunately, he stopped sliding after a few inches.

It was a fairly tight squeeze under the seat. Perhaps the woman in front was right, Ziggy thought. Perhaps I am a mental retard. I must be to be going through all this. Still he was on his way, and no matter how uncomfortable he felt, he was not going to push his luck any further. He was going to stay under that seat until they landed at Manchester. He only hoped he wouldn't be too stiff to climb out when they got there!!

FIFTEEN

As Ziggy took off for Manchester, Gonch and Hollo still had their feet well and truly on earth, if not a few feet below it. And for the past hour they had also been below a few extra feet. Two belonging to Mr Griffiths and six others belonging to the local police!

'What time is it now?' Gonch whispered.

Hollo pressed the button on his digital watch. 'Just gone half-eight.'

'Can you hear anything?'

Hollo shook his head. It had been quiet for about ten minutes.

'God knows what me mum'll be thinking,' whispered Gonch.

'Mine too.'

'She doesn't mind up until about seven. Gets a bit ratty like, but she's used to me coming in late. I'll really get it at this time, though.'

'Me too,' Hollo whispered glumly.

'Just glad I was able to snatch this back.' He held up his Walkman. 'At least I'll only get it in the neck for being in late. Not losing this.'

'Do you think it's safe yet?' Hollo whispered.

'Give it a couple of minutes.'

Hollo nodded and settled down on the floor of the duct. It was filthy and dusty but he didn't care. He just didn't want to get caught.

They had both nearly died on the spot when the alarm bells started to ring. For an instant they hadn't realised what the noise was. Then they realised. Of course. The school had to have a burglar alarm system. Then panic, as they realised the police would be there in minutes.

They had both dived back into the manhole in the corridor. Hollo had been reaching for the cover when Gonch had jumped up and dashed into the Staff Room.

'Gonch! What are you doing?' Hollo had called.

'Getting this!' Gonch had answered as he came running back with his Walkman in his hand. 'If I don't get it now, I won't be able to later, will I?' Gonch jumped into the duct and helped Hollo pull the cover back into place.

It had probably been longer, but it had seemed almost instantaneously that they had heard the nah-nah-nah-nah of the police sirens – then heavy footsteps and shouting as people came running along the corridor, right on top of the heating duct. It was difficult to make out any sounds through the concrete cover, but they had been able to recognise the unmistakeable voice of old Griffiths. The police were moaning that it was a false alarm. Old Griffiths had finally agreed that he couldn't see any signs of damage, or any signs of anyone breaking in.

Gonch and Hollo had held their breath through all this. They hadn't really thought anyone standing above could have heard them, but they had just felt safer not moving. They had also been holding their breath in hope that no one went round to the boiler room and noticed the lock broken on the old coal chute.

For an hour they hadn't dared to move, even when Hollo was convinced there was a rat crawling up his trouser leg. (It turned out to be an itch on the back of his leg – he was glad he hadn't said anything to Gonch.)

For an hour they had waited for some sign that the boiler room chute had been discovered. But there was nothing. Now there was no noise from above, no indication of movement. Old Griffiths and Old Bill seem to have gone home. Another false alarm in the record books.

After another couple of minutes silence, Hollo eventually whispered, 'What do you reckon?'

'They've gone,' replied Gonch. He twisted round and re-lit the candle. Even in its meagre light the two lads looked filthy.

'What now, then?'

'Out. As fast as we can!'

'How? The candle won't last long. And we were lost before all this, remember?'

'I know that, duck brain. But what do you think I've been doing lying here. Peeing in me pants for an hour?'

Hollo just pulled a 'very funny' face, which was lost in the darkness. He said, 'Well? What?'

'We're outside the Staff Room, right?'

'You should be on Mastermind, do you know that?'

Gonch let it pass. 'This corridor runs straight along the main building, doesn't it?' Hollo nodded. 'Then it turns right by the History Room. Pass the Assembly Hall and what have you got on your left?'

Hollo thought. He couldn't remember. 'The bogs.'

'Past those, clown.'

'Er . . . oh . . . yeah.' Now he realised what Gonch was saying. 'The Woodwork room.'

'Right,' said Gonch. 'Behind which is the boiler

room. All we've got to do is follow that same route and we'll be there. Right?'

'Right!' said Hollo, cheering up at the idea of escape.

'C'mon,' said Gonch, already twisting round to face in the right direction. As he did the candle died, and so did Hollo's hope. He hesitated.

'What now?'

'We carry on.'

'In the dark?'

'No. We'll sit here and wait for someone to come along with a torch.'

Gonch went to move, but Hollo stopped him.

'What if this duct doesn't follow the corridor exactly, like?'

Gonch paused for a moment. 'We can't get out through the school, can we? In case we set off more alarms. They've probably got all the doors and windows wired up. Right?'

'Right.'

'The boiler room is the only way out. These ducts go to the boiler room and we got here through them. Right?'

'Right.'

'We've got to do something. Our parents will be going mental by now and you haven't got any better ideas. Right?'

Hollo hesitated. Gonch was right. Yet again.

'C'mon, then,' said Gonch.

'Right!' said Hollo, and followed.

Hollo may not have had any better ideas, but it didn't take him long to realise that they were in trouble. After about five metres he heard Gonch swear and then start to moan and groan in pain.

'Aagghh . . . orrgghh . . . oowww,' cried Gonch. He had crawled straight into a concrete wall.

As Gonch lay on the floor rubbing his head in agony, Hollo slowly crawled forward and felt his way around the duct. They were at a junction. The duct did not follow the path of the corridor above it. It branched off in two opposite directions. One left. One right.

'We'll never find our way out now, will we?' Hollo groaned.

'Course we will.'

'How? We got lost with the candle. We'll never get out in the dark.'

'We know the layout of the school, don't we? We can work it out. I reckon we're right outside McCluskey's office.'

'Yeah. But you're only guessing because you know it's along the corridor from the Staff Room.'

'So? So long as we keep working out where we are we should be OK.'

'We won't, Gonch. We won't. We might know the layout of the school. But this doesn't follow the same layout. We'll soon get lost again. And we were lucky to find that manhole open, weren't we? If we lose that, we might never get out!'

Hollo was beginning to panic. Gonch could feel it – it was in his voice. Not that he blamed him. He felt a bit like that himself. But he knew there had to be a way out.

'Let's go back to that manole,' Hollo pleaded.

'And do what?' Gonch almost laughed.

'See if we can get out through the school.'

'We won't. We'll set the alarms off again.'

'So. We can be away before anyone gets here!'

108

'And what if we're not? What if Griffiths or even the police are sitting outside? What about our fingerprints? They'd be all over the place! They already are on the Staff Room door. Well, mine are anyway. If they think there's been a real break-in they'll go looking for things like that won't they?' Gonch couldn't see Hollo's face, but he could sense that he was nodding agreement. 'And what would happen to us then? It wouldn't just be a slagging off our mum and dad for being out late. It'll be the whole law business, won't it? Done for breaking in and expelled from school, probably. Right?'

Hollo didn't answer, but Gonch needed him to answer, so that he knew he was not on his own in the escape plan. 'Well. Am I right?'

'Yeah,' muttered Hollo. 'Yeah. But I just can't see how we're going to get out of here.'

As he said it, neither could Gonch. If only we *had* brought some string or some chalk, he thought. We could have left a trail behind us. We could have followed it out, though chalk wouldn't have been much good in the dark, would it. We could have felt our way along a piece of string. Still, no sense thinking about something we didn't do or haven't got. Or have we? It suddenly hit him. He didn't have any string but he had something that might do.

Quickly he pulled the Walkman from his pocket and pressed the eject button. The cassette was still there. It was his favourite compilation tape but he didn't care. He could make another. He put the cassette back in the machine and pressed the rewind button. He wanted all the tape on one reel.

'What are you doing?' Hollo asked. He could hear Gonch fiddling with the Walkman.

'We can use the cassette.'

'What for?'

'If we cut the tape and tie one end to one of these pipes, we can let it run out behind as we go. That way, although we might get a bit lost, we'll always know if we're doubling back on ourselves. Or going somewhere we've been before. Right?'

'Yeah. Right. Right. Right. Let's go,' said Hollo, filled with renewed hope.

'Hang on. I've got to rewind the tape. Looks like someone's been listening to it since they confiscated it off me.'

'Probably Bronson,' offered Hollo.

They both laughed. The very thought of Bronson listening to rock music was enough to bring a smile to their faces. The Walkman clicked as the cassette stopped. Gonch pulled it out, and fished out the tape with his front door key. He snapped it and tied it to a pipe bracket. 'Now, let's go.'

'Which way?'

'Er . . . the boiler room is to the right. So right it is. Right?'

'Right. But er . . . do us a favour, Gonch?'

'What?'

'Stop saying right?' Hollo asked.

'Er . . . right! I mean OK.' The two mates laughed. With spirits restored they set off.

Amazingly enough it worked. It took them half an hour. They got lost a couple of times and found they were crossing over the tape twice, but eventually they found their way back to the boiler room. There was one nasty moment when the tape ran out and they didn't think they would make it.

They were still in the ducts in total darkness when

it happened. They were just about to panic when fortunately Hollo found the puddle he had crawled through earlier. This meant they were only just round a corner from the boiler room.

They scrambled out of the duct, through the boiler room and up the old coal chute. No one had discovered the broken lock. They practically dived out into the fresh air, dashed across the playground, past the bin enclosure and didn't stop running until they had passed the dead cat in the subway and were sitting on the wall behind the pensioners' flats. There they stopped to get their breath back. That was when they realised what a real state they were in. They looked like they had been down the mines. They had escaped from one danger, but now faced an even greater one. What would they tell their parents they had been doing to get in such a mess? Never mind where they had been until nine o'clock!

SIXTEEN

Gonch and Hollo had had their lucky escape but was
Ziggy going to manage his? At the moment he
couldn't move. He felt the plane land. He felt the
bumps as it touched down on the runway. He knew
he had to get out from beneath the seat, ready to mix
with all the other passengers as they got off the plane.
He knew he had to do it. But he still couldn't move.

Ziggy remembered back to falling on the walkway.
His legs wouldn't move then, but this was different.
His whole body was stiff. It had gone numb. He was
convinced he had nearly died on the way. He was
sure he had put so much strain on his heart sneaking
through Heathrow and on to the plane, that it was
unable to keep his blood circulating when he was
squashed under the seat.

He remembered losing the feeling in his legs even
before the cabin staff started serving drinks. He lost
his arms somewhere over Birmingham. He knew it
was Birmingham because the pilot had told them over
the loudspeakers. The weather was fine and he hoped
they were all comfortable and enjoying their flight.
Ziggy guessed the pilot's message was not aimed at
people travelling squashed under the seats.

The only part of his body that Ziggy could feel was
his back. Perhaps it was the way it was jammed up
against the seat legs, or just simply the position he
was in, but Ziggy's back was now really hurting. It
hadn't hurt like this for days. In fact he had hardly

noticed it since he started out on this incredible journey. But now it was stinging like mad.

Still, that was not his main problem. He had to get some movement back so he could get out from under the seat. He didn't want to have come so far, only to be found by a cleaner hoovering under the rows. He concentrated on his right arm. It was the one on top. He tried to move it. It wouldn't budge. He tried again. Nothing. It was completely dead. He tried his other arm. Same thing.

Flippin' 'eck, groaned Ziggy as he tried once again. I hope I'm not permanently crippled. Come on, arm. Move, will you. Suddenly his arm did move – just an inch or two and then it stopped. Ziggy began to panic. He was beginning to wonder what life as a cripple would be like, when he noticed his sleeve was hooked on the underside of the seat cushion. He wasn't crippled, only snagged on the seat.

Slowly Ziggy pulled himself out from beneath row 27. As he did he could feel the plane begin to stop.

Already people were beginning to stand up, collect their bags and jam the aisle. Exactly what Ziggy wanted. The only problem was he wasn't sure his legs would support him. He forced himself to stand. It was painful. His knees wobbled. He could feel the pins and needles starting in his feet. It was like having socks full of glass, as he started to walk toward the door at the front of the plane.

He didn't know where to go but reckoned the best thing to do was to follow the crowd. As he stepped off the plane he got a funny look off one of the stewardesses, but he forced himself to smile. Act natural. Ordinary. Normal. To his surprise she smiled back.

He went down the steps and into the airport

building, all the time trying to appear to be with someone — especially as he reached the end of the corridor where there was a security check point. Ziggy's fears came flooding back. He started to wonder if they had radioed ahead. Would they seize him now? With his stiff legs he was walking in a rather peculiar way, and he was bound to be obvious.

However, nothing happened. No one even looked at him. But why should they? The security is there to stop the wrong people getting on, not getting off. He looked round. He couldn't believe it. He saw the sign 'WELCOME TO MANCHESTER'. He was in the main airport building. He had done the impossible.

Yeah, thought Ziggy, I made it to Manchester. But how do I get to Liverpool? He noticed an Information Booth at the far end of the building, and he hobbled along as fast as his pins and needles could carry him.

'Are you sure?' he heard himself asking the girl behind the desk.

'Quite sure. There is no train to Liverpool. You'd have to go into Manchester city centre first.'

Ziggy was going to ask how he could do that, how long it would take and how much it would cost, but didn't. He just nodded and walked away. He was too tired. He didn't want to travel any more. Every part of his body now ached. His back was stinging like mad. He was ready to give up again. He saw a row of seats and flopped down on one.

He leant forward, his elbows on his knees, like he had on the tube train on his way home from Euston. It seemed so long ago. He felt like crying. He didn't quite know why. It wasn't the pains in his legs, or his back. He wasn't really scared any more. He just felt so upset. He was almost there but not quite. Stranded

114

in Manchester. Without the will to move on. He felt as though he was going to cry. So he bit his lip. Come on, he said to himself. Come on, bone brain. You've come all this way. Don't give up now. He looked across at another digital clock. 21.30.

Half past nine. Even if I could afford to go into Manchester it'd probably take me until well after eleven o'clock until I got to Liverpool. I'd end up getting home too late. I may be in Manchester but I'm right back in the same position I was before. It's all been a waste of time. A bloody waste of time. But even if it was, I've still got to get to Liverpool to get the train back tonight in case me ma . . . he stopped. In case me ma has noticed I'm missing. She might have done by now, mightn't she. And if she has they'll all be at Lime Street station by now. He stood up and looked for a phone. He'd phone his Auntie Ann.

I'll do the same as before, he thought as he dropped his money into the coin box. I'll say I'm still phoning to speak to Allie. If me ma hasn't found out I'll speak to her. Tell her where I am. She'll sort it out for me. If mum has found out, they'll be glad to know I'm OK. As he dialled the number he wondered what his mum would be like if she had found out. It sent a shiver down his spine.

Burr-burr. Burr-burr. Burr-burr. The phone kept ringing. 'Come on. Come on,' muttered Ziggy as he danced from one foot to another. 'Come on. Answer the phone.'

Burr-burr. Still no response. 'Bloody hell,' Ziggy swore. All this way. All this effort. And there's no one in. He went to slam down the phone but caught it, just in time. He'd heard something. 'Hello?' he enquired into the receiver.

'Hello. Who's that?' a voice asked from the other end. Ziggy recognised it. It was Allison.

'Hi, Allie. It's me.'

'Rick? Is that you?'

'Course it's me, idiot.' Ziggy felt like crying again, this time with joy. It was so good to hear her voice. He could picture her standing in Auntie Ann's hall, her long hair falling over the phone as she put it to her ear.

'Where are you? Whose phone are you using?'

'It's a call-box. Did er . . . did Auntie Ann tell you I phoned earlier, like?'

'No. We've only just come in. She's out. Listen, kidder. Why are you phoning?'

Ziggy noticed that she said 'we've' only just come in. That meant she was with Dopey Dennis. 'I er . . . I just wanted to talk to you.' Ziggy wanted to tell her how much he missed her. How much he'd like to fall asleep on her knee again. Feel her long hair. But he couldn't. He felt embarrassed about it.

'What about? You OK.?' Allison asked. She could sense something was not quite natural. Not ordinary. Not normal. 'Where are you, Rick?'

'I'm er . . . I'm er. . . .' I'd better tell her, he thought. I'd better.

'Where?' she insisted.

'Manchester,' he muttered. 'Well, Manchester Airport.'

'What are you doing there?' She sounded shocked.

'Wondering exactly the same thing meself.' He tried to laugh, but it got no response from the other end. It was silent. 'I was er . . . lonely, Al.'

'Were you?' she finally asked, although he couldn't tell whether it was a genuine or sarcastic question.

'Yeah.'

116

'What about me mum?'

'She doesn't know. I left her a note, though.'

'Bloody hell, Rick. How did you get there? Where did you get the money from?' Allison fired off the questions as it all began to sink in. Her brother had flown up from London.

'I, er . . . it's a long story. But . . . but I was lonely. I . . . er – missed you, like. You know. . . .' There, he had said it. He didn't care any more.

It seemed to do the trick. She calmed down. 'Hang on a minute,' she said. He heard her cover the phone with her hand and say something to someone. Probably Dopey Dennis.

'What's going on, Al?' he demanded.

'Hang on a minute, I said.'

Ziggy did hang on for a minute. And a bit more before Allison came back on the line. 'Where exactly are you in the airport?'

'Er . . . by the Information Desk thingy.'

'Right. Don't move. I'll be over in half an hour.'

Ziggy's heart jumped, this time from excitement, not fright. 'Will you?' he asked.

'Yeah. Dennis will run me over in his car.'

'Oh . . . OK.' That was a less exciting prospect, thought Ziggy. At least she was coming. She would sort everything out for him. 'See you soon,' he said into the phone as the pips began to go.

'Stay exactly where you are!' was the last thing he heard Allison say before the phone cut off. He put it back on its cradle. Don't worry, he thought. I've had enough travelling for one night. He looked up at the clock. 21.40. Even his arms and legs felt better now. She would be here in half an hour. She would hold him. He could feel her hair. She would make everything all right.

SEVENTEEN

It was nearly half past ten. Gonch and Hollo were home and in bed. Ziggy was still waiting for his sister Allison, and wishing he were home in bed. Laura was already asleep, but Julia was still trying. She couldn't sleep. She kept thinking about what a close call she had had with her father.

The girls had been right. The ride home had been unpleasant. No one had spoken, not even when they dropped Laura off. Julia's father had not said a word. She had dashed into the house and straight up to her bedroom where she sat on her bed and listened to him going through the ritual of parking the car. He'd be up soon, she had thought. God, why did I listen to Laura? Why?

Of course there was no answer to that question. There never was. Even by the time Julia heard him coming up the stairs, she still hadn't found a good enough reason. Where should she say she'd been? Should she tell more lies? No, she decided. No. I listened to Laura and look where that ended up, she thought. She decided to tell the truth.

As the door opened she took a deep breath, waiting for her father's anger to flow in and fill the room. It didn't. He was quite calm. He was holding the cigarette box from the Jumble Sale which she'd left on the back seat of the car. 'Where did you get this?' he asked.

She took another deep breath. 'I bought it. At a Jumble Sale.'

'St Saviour's?' he asked.

'Er . . . yes,' Julia had replied. She was astonished to see her father nod and walk out of the room. How did he know? What had happened? Where had he gone?

The answer was provided about five minutes later when Julia's mother came up to see if she was all right. Of course she was, she had told her mother, but what had happened to her father? Julia's mother had sat on the bed and told her.

Some years before, her father had bought a similar cigarette box as a present for his brother, Julia's Uncle Max. Uncle Max lived near St Saviour's Church. Julia had guessed what was in her father's mind. Had Uncle Max given the cigarette box to the Jumble Sale? Her mother had told her that her father had gone to phone Uncle Max. He had. He'd given the cigarette box away. He also told her father what he'd heard had happened at the Jumble Sale, although he didn't actually know it was Julia who had thrown the trifle. Julia told her mother it was, and it was this that had taken the wind out of Julia's father's sails. He now knew where Julia had been and it hadn't seemed to matter. He was more upset about his brother giving away the cigarette box. Julia felt sorry for him. What a miserable thing to do, she kept thinking. To give away such a beautiful present.

Her mother went down after extracting a promise from Julia that she wouldn't lie like that again, and Julia readily promised. She knew she wouldn't be so lucky the next time, if there was a next time. Oh well, she thought as she finally drifted off to sleep, I'm just glad I got away with it tonight. Perhaps the vicar of

119

St Saviour's was right. Perhaps God had been kind to us.

God may have been kind to Julia, but he was brilliant to Gonch and Hollo.

They had sat on top of the pensioners' wall for about fifteen minutes trying to get their breath back. They were also trying to think of a plausible story to explain why they both looked like they'd been dragged up from the bottom of the canal. By the time old Mrs Bimpson had spotted them and started shouting at them to clear off before she called the police, Gonch had decided it would be safer if they both killed themselves. Even then his mum wouldn't be upset. She'd be annoyed that he was stupid enough to do it.

Gonch had the idea when they were climbing down the telephone box.

'We'll phone up,' he said.

'We'll what?'

'We'll phone up and crack on that we've been to . . . er . . . been to Billy Mack's,' Gonch suggested.

'I don't like Billy Mack,' Hollo protested.

'I know that. Neither do I, do I?' Gonch said. 'But our mums don't know that, do they?'

'Well, what good will that do us?'

'He's got a trail bike, hasn't he?'

'Yeah. So what?'

'So. We say we've been having a go. Got carried away and got scruffed up.'

'Oh, great, that is. Me mum'll still kill me,' Hollo moaned.

'No, she won't,' Gonch told him. 'She'll only half-kill you for that. She'd kill you if you told her you'd just bust into the school.'

Hollo had thought about it. It was the best solution. 'But what about the phone bit?'

'Just a gamble,' he said. 'Try and pretend we've been phoning all night. Say the phone's been broken.'

Hollo looked at him. Then grabbed Goncho's head and kissed his forehead. 'You're a genius.'

'I know,' Gonch had replied in his usual modest way.

Gonch was not only a genius that night, he was lucky, too – and so was Hollo. When they phoned they had received no answer from Gonch's, and at Hollo's his older brother Michael had answered. His mum and dad were out. His dad had gone to play snooker and his mum had gone out to a Jumble Sale. They had both gone about seven and had not been too worried about where he was. His mum had phoned about eight and his brother had lied, saying he was in. Great. Good old Mike. He'd been through it all before. He wanted to know where Hollo was as he had been starting to worry himself. Hollo told him he'd be there in ten minutes. He had made it in six and was washed and changed in nine. One minute later his mum had walked in.

Gonch's mum arrived at about the same time as Hollo's mum got home. They had both been to the same Jumble Sale. She came through the front door to find a very comfortable Gonch, washed and changed into his jeans and a sweat shirt. 'What time did you get in?' his mum asked, taking off her blue woollen coat.

'Oh ... er ... about half-seven.' He decided it

121

would be best to be on the safe side.

'And where were you till then?'

'Went over to Billy Mack's,' Gonch said. Might as well keep the story to cover the dirty clothes, he thought. 'Fancy a cup of tea?' he asked calmly. That was always good when she came in, a bit of sympathy.

'Oh, yes, thanks, love,' his mum said. 'My right foot's killing me. Some toffee-nosed girl stood on it at the Jumble Sale.'

'Oh ... yeah. I saw your note. St Saviour's, was it?' Gonch asked. Laura had been right. Everyone did support St Saviour's, and Gonch was *very* lucky that night.

'Yeah. Sorry I didn't phone. I was going to, but, well there was quite a bit of excitement there. Someone tried to steal the raffle money. Broke in through a toilet window, someone said.'

'Straight up?' Gonch was genuinely interested, but the mention of breaking-in had reminded him of his own exploits. And about its purpose. 'Oh ... er ... by the way ... look. Before you ask.'

'What?' she looked puzzled for a moment. Until she saw him pointing at his Walkman. 'Oh that, I'd forgotten all about that. Look at the state of my tights. That girl has ruined them.'

Gonch felt sick. He couldn't accept that he'd gone through all he had for nothing. The very night his mum wasn't going to ask about his Walkman. 'And that reminds me,' his mum went on. 'The school has sent me a form to fill in for the insurance on the other one you had stolen. They need it tomorrow.'

Even now as he lay in bed staring at the insurance

form on the floor beside his bed, Gonch couldn't believe he'd heard his mum correctly. He realised what it all meant. When he took the insurance form to school tomorrow, the staff were bound to comment about his other Walkman being confiscated. They would notice it was missing. They would be told of the burglar alarms going off. Griffiths would be bound to find the broken lock on the boiler room. They would search for fingerprints. If the only thing missing in the break-in was his Walkman, who would they suspect? Whose fingerprints would they want to check?

Oh no, moaned Gonch. He swung out of bed and crept along the landing. Mum was listening to the radio as she did some ironing downstairs. He sneaked into her bedroom and picked up the phone extension. He dialled. After a moment Hollo answered. 'Hollo,' Gonch whispered. 'Remember when you said you came with me tonight because it wouldn't be much fun without you? Well . . .' Gonch took a breath. 'I've got to put the Walkman back in the Staff Room.' The phone went dead. Hollo had hung up. Gonch wondered why.

If nothing had happened as expected for Julia, Gonch and Hollo, Ziggy was no exception. Things had started to go wrong. Allison should have collected him by now. She wasn't here. The digital clock flicked over. 23.34. She'd said she would only be half an hour – that was when the digital clock showed 21.40. He had watched it change 54 times since then. 54 minutes. Where was she? He wanted to see her.

He looked at the clock again. 22.41. His back was

really giving him aggravation now. I must have really knocked it or something under that seat, he thought. When I get home I'm not getting out of me bed until it's healed properly. I don't care what happens. He was twisting himself about, waving his arms and moving his shoulders up and down, trying to ease the itching, when the next unexpected – and yet obvious – thing happened. A security guard was standing in front of him. 'What are you up to, then?' the man asked.

Ziggy felt his heart thump. He looked at the security guard. Does he know, he wondered. Has he been watching me and figured out what I've done?

'How'd you mean, like?' replied Ziggy.

'What are you doing here? Bit young to be out by yourself, aren't you?'

Ziggy had been right. He was too conspicuous by himself. 'Er . . . I'm waiting for me sister to come and collect me. She should have been here by now.' Keep as close to the truth as possible, thought Ziggy. Be natural. Ordinary. Normal.

'Should she now? Where's she coming from?'

'Liverpool.'

'Bit of a distance, isn't it?'

'Yeah . . . er . . . about 38 miles, I think,' Ziggy replied with a smile. It seemed to be the wrong answer. The guard seemed more curious.

'How did you get here?'

'By plane. It's an airport, isn't it?' He couldn't help it. It just came out. He knew he'd blown it. He'd antagonised the guard. All this way and I've blown it. He's going to ask me what airline I came on.

'What airline did you come in on?'

'The shuttle from London,' Ziggy replied. I've got to get away from here, he thought. He'll want to see me ticket next. Then I've had it. He decided to try and divert the guard. 'I've been to see me Auntie. She paid for it an' all. Down there. At Heathrow.'

'Did she?' the guard asked. 'So you won't mind me seeing your ticket then, will you?'

Ziggy's heart jumped this time. This was it. Caught. He hesitated. Looked for a way to run. The guard took a step nearer. Ziggy put his hands in his pockets.

'Er . . . can't er . . can't find it,' he said, as he found the torn boarding card. Would that do? 'There's the er . . . boarding card thing.'

'But where's the ticket?' the guard asked. He's not going to give up. He's got me, thought Ziggy. Where's Allie? Why didn't she come when she said? Why wasn't she here making everything all right? His train of thought was stopped dead by a girl's voice.

'Rick? What's going on?' It was Allison's voice.

With great relief he turned round, but found the next unexpected thing. She had short hair. And it was blonde. Her long black hair was gone. 'Al?' he asked, as though to make sure.

'Idiot!' she said as she pulled him to her and hugged him.

'Owww!' he cried as she hugged his back.

'Oh, sorry. I forgot. Mum told me about it!'

For a moment her remark didn't register. He was slowing down. Even if Allison had cut her hair she still felt as soft and warm as usual. Everything would be all right now. It was only when she had pulled him away from the security guard and outside to Dopey Dennis's car that the hairs on Ziggy's neck stood on end. Mum told her. When? When had she told her? When?

It may also have had something to do with the punch Allison aimed at his head. 'What was that for?' Ziggy demanded. 'You know what it's for. It's for coming here. Or the way you came here. Idiot.' She hit him again. His back hit the car. It stung like mad.

'Ah, hey, Al . . .' he tried to protest.

'Don't! Just don't speak to me. Get in the car.'

He did. Dopey didn't say a word. He never did. 'Does me ma really know?' Ziggy asked.

'Of course she does. You don't think I wouldn't tell her, do you? You can't be that much of an idiot!' As she spoke she turned in her seat to face him and Ziggy saw something that convinced him she was right. He *was* an idiot. The whole thing had been stupid from start to finish. Allison was wearing a 'Wham!' sweatshirt! He shook his head. Allie liking 'Wham!' He just couldn't believe it.

After a few minutes he spoke again.

'What sort of state is me ma in?' he asked.

What do you think?' (He could imagine.) 'But she told me to tell you one thing. You're to stay overnight. But then straight home tomorrow. And straight to school. If your back's well enough to fly it's well enough to go back to school.'

That sounded like me ma, Ziggy thought. Still, can't blame her, can I? As they drove away from the airport a holiday jet took off. He twisted to look at it and in so doing realised he still had the cotton wool and tissues stuffed in his pocket. He pulled them out and looked at the plane's flashing lights in the dark night sky. Then his face broke into a huge grin.

There'd be no more after-hours adventures for him for a long time. But it had still been better than lying in his bed all alone. And he would still get to see the girls.